HOPE'S PEAK

TONY HEALEY

A HARPER AND LANE MYSTERY

 THOMAS & MERCER

Culture Perth and Kinross Ltd.	
05770495	
Askews & Holts	Mar-2017
AF HEA	£8.99

Text copyright © 2017 by Tony Healey

Published by Thomas & Mercer, Seattle

www.apub.com

Amazon, the Amazon logo, and Thomas & Mercer are trademarks of Amazon.com, Inc., or its affiliates.

ISBN-13: 9781503940956
ISBN-10: 1503940950

Cover design by Cyanotype Book Architects

Printed in the United States of America

For Lesley

1

The tall corn rustles like paper. The young woman lies flat on the dry earth, arms by her sides, feet together, chin resting on her chest; her head is propped up against the thick green stalks. Her eyes are closed—at first glance, you could be forgiven for thinking she's asleep.

Detective Jane Harper squats next to the body. "How old?" she asks, looking up at the medical examiner. "Late teens?"

Mike McNeil, the medical examiner, rubs at the gray stubble on his jaw. "I won't know for sure till I get her back to the office, but I'd say so, yeah."

There are purple handprints around her neck—the killer left his mark when he crushed her windpipe. A troubled frown is forever etched into the girl's brow, a lasting impression of terror.

Wondering what's happening . . . and why *it's happening to* her.

Mike shifts from one foot to the other, the keys on his belt jingling. It's off-putting.

Harper points to the red spread of blood on the girl's white cotton dress, over her groin. "Raped. Like the last one."

"Could be," Mike says. He sighs, and Harper can't tell if it's from the oppressive nature of the crime scene itself or the fact that she's holding him up from doing his job—could be either or both.

The young woman has a crown of twisted vine on her head. It has been hand fashioned, each woody twig intertwined with the next. Here and there leaves poke out. When the first victim was found, Harper had the crown on the girl's head tested. It was identified as supplejack vine, native to the Carolinas. She has no doubt this one is the same—it appears to be.

She rubs the earth between her fingertips before getting up. "Ground's dry. Sorta dusty. Forensics might be able to get something from it."

"Hopefully," Mike says, though his tone suggests otherwise.

The sun's already turning the air to a hot, cloying soup, and Harper's eager to get out of the corn. "Alright, Mike. Do what you do best."

She walks back through the corn, snapping off her rubber gloves. Where the corn ends, the road is closed; the boys in blue deal with the few locals who've stopped by to see what's up. The locals stand right up against the yellow tape stretched across the road, asking questions the officers on duty refuse to answer with anything more than grunts.

Harper adjusts her shades and ignores the spectators gathered at the cordoning tape. Detective Stu Raley waits for her, tie already loosened around his neck, leaning back against the side of his car. He is six feet, has blond hair, a strong chin, and has maintained the muscular build he developed in the army.

"You look flustered, Jane," Stu says.

She nods grimly. "I could say the same about *you*. Got my message?"

"An hour ago. I came straight out."

"You want to see the body before it's moved?" an officer asks him.

"In a minute," Stu says, turning to Harper. "I thought I'd catch you first, see if you needed anything."

"Figures," Harper says, managing a smile. "I know you're never in a hurry for gore this time of the morning . . ."

"Ain't that the truth?" Stu makes a face, his hand on his sternum. "Anyway, I'm building myself up to it."

"Don't worry, I got it covered," Harper says. "Crime Scene Unit's on the way. Mike's going to get the body out of here once they turn up and do their thing."

"Think they'll pull something new?"

"Perhaps. She *is* in better condition than the last one," Harper says, feeling dirty for referring to a dead person as a *thing*, an inanimate object. When you're dealing with dead teenage girls, the only way to cope with what you see, with what you know, is to detach yourself. It helps to have a disconnect.

Think of that dead young woman as an object *and maybe you won't end up in a loony bin.*

"Here." Stu hands her a cup of coffee. "Drank mine on the way over."

"Thanks." Harper stands next to him, her back to the car, looking into the swaying corn. The gray road, the green field, the pale-pink sky turning to faded blue, the black girl . . . the killer's handprints on her throat, the red blossom on her white dress.

Harper lifts the lid off the coffee and sips it.

"Second body in three months," Stu says. "Same MO, too?"

"Yeah, looks like it."

Stu faces her. "Hey."

"Yeah?"

"Either it's a coincidence the killer's murdered a second black girl, or . . ."

Harper sets the coffee cup on the roof of the car and runs her fingers through her hair. "Or he's purposely setting out to kill black girls of a certain age and type, and we're dealing with a fledgling serial killer."

"There's a big possibility," Stu says.

"You know what really gets me about this guy?" Harper asks. "The way he closes their eyes."

Stu shakes his head, eyes narrowed. "Maybe he's ashamed and can't stand 'em looking back at him."

Harper doesn't tell him she's already considered the prospect. "Any word on our witness?"

In the early hours, a delivery driver saw a man walk out of the corn, completely naked except for a white mask. A truck was parked twenty yards farther down the road. The driver called it in right away, using his GPS to give them the location—it's the first break they've had with the case so far, if you don't figure the killer's DNA into the equation, taken from the previous victim. But even that proved a dead end. The Combined DNA Index System contains only *known* offenders—if the perpetrator has never been caught and booked, he's not in CODIS— and that's about as useful as having fingerprints for someone who's never had their prints catalogued.

"The driver's at the station. I asked him to wait."

"Thanks, I appreciate that," Harper says. "I'll bet Dudley was chomping at the bit to get in there."

"He can go kiss my ass." Stu smiles. "If Dudley thinks he's making lieutenant on the back of our work, he's wrong. I asked Albie to hold the fort till you get there."

"Oh, you're not coming along?"

"The captain's got me interviewing the farmer who works these fields, see if he knows anything. Owen Willard owns all this. I don't think I'll be long."

Harper turns to face Stu and straightens his tie. He looks at her the way he does when they lie in bed after a few beers, listening to her talk, one arm under his pillow, the other around her waist. It's all she can do to look away, thinking of the broken girl in that sea of corn.

The Crime Scene Unit arrives in a white van. Harper pats the side of Stu's face and goes to greet them. "I guess this is me. Thanks for the coffee, stud."

"Anytime, kiddo."

She glances back to see him walk across the road and into the corn. The shifting green stems part and swallow her partner whole.

In the little apartment Harper rents over a tackle shop in the middle of Hope's Peak, she has a board on the wall. It's something she started doing back in San Francisco, when she worked on her first big case—a rapist the papers christened "The Moth." On the board, the case is a sprawl of information: the newspaper clippings relating to the murder of the first victim, a map of the local area, a pin holding a torn scrap of paper with **MAGNOLIA REMY** scrawled on it. Later, Harper will go to her apartment and tack another name to the board—she hopes beyond hope that it will *not* be **JANE DOE**.

When she arrives at the station, Detective John Dudley waits by the interview room. Detective Albert Goode is inside talking to the witness. "Ready to rock and roll?" Dudley asks her.

"Yeah," Harper says stiffly. "But this is *my* investigation; I'll question him with Goode, okay?"

He eyes her suspiciously. Opens his mouth to say something, but she cuts him off.

"It's the way it is, Dudley."

The detective shrugs. "Whatever. Your investigation. Your rules," he says and walks off. When the first girl was found, Captain Morelli put the team together. Stu Raley and Harper running lead, with Dudley and Goode for support, much to Dudley's displeasure.

Albie gets up, holds the door for her—he's learning the ropes fast and is tougher than he seems, despite his soft voice and pleasant disposition. Harper doesn't get the impression Captain Morelli is too keen on Albie. But when Morelli was younger, it was a white-male-dominated workplace. The times have changed.

The trucker pushes himself up from his chair, but Harper waves him down.

"No need to get up."

"Man, I got a run to make. My foreman's gonna go nuts."

"I understand that," Harper says. "I won't take up too much of your time."

"Hope not. I mean, I'm all for doing the right thing, but I've pretty much lost a day's pay for this shit."

A dead girl. A murder, Harper thinks. *This shit.*

She sits down, starts the recorder. "Detective Jane Harper with Detective Albert Goode interviewing eyewitness Nate Filch." She checks the time and date, saying it aloud for the purpose of the recording.

"We really appreciate you doing this," Albie says. "And for being patient."

The trucker looks less than happy. He runs his fingers through his thinning hair. She guesses him to be in his early thirties. A few crummy tattoos up his arms, holes in earlobes where he used to have piercings.

Harper begins: "So, tell us where you were headed so early this morning."

"Stock run. I work for Tripper's Destinations. They supply about five hundred businesses around here, dotted all over the place. I drive for 'em, delivering."

"Where are they based?"

"Farther north. Look, I already told you guys all this . . ."

Harper leans forward slightly, enough to get his attention. "This is for the official record. What you say here, we'll use to solve a very serious crime. It's important we cover every detail, and that you be accurate to the best of your knowledge. Okay?"

"Right."

Albie clears his throat. "Okay. So you're heading down that road. It's nighttime?"

"Yeah. It's dark, I'm rollin' a cigarette while I hold the wheel. Ya know, the way ya do sometimes? The road's clear, empty, the radio's on. I can't remember what was playing, though . . ."

Albie looks at Harper. "It's not important," he tells the trucker. "Go on."

"So anyway, I'm rollin' this cigarette, and just happen to look farther up. The headlights land on this thing walkin' into the road. I think, *Shit!*, like it's a deer or something like that? Drivin' at night you just get in the zone, man. It takes me a second to realize it's a guy, lookin' straight at me."

"Let's slow it down a bit here," Harper says. "Describe the man."

Nate Filch blows air from the side of his mouth as he tries to remember. "Maybe six feet and a bit, tall gangly fella, completely buck naked."

Harper asks, "Did you see any blood?"

Filch nods, hand on his abdomen. "Looked like he had a load of it around *here*."

"Okay. Did he carry a weapon that you could see?"

"Don't know. The guy had nothin' in his hands, so guess not."

"What about his head? You mentioned a mask of some kind?"

"What he was wearin', it was like . . . a *bag*. A white sheet, maybe a pillowcase, with the eyes cut out. You know, to see from. Looked to me like he had a belt around his neck, holdin' it in place. The way it was around his head, though, it looked like a white bag."

Albie frowns. "When you say a white sheet . . ."

"Like the KKK, okay fella? Big enough to cover his head. Looked like a fuckin' ghost, man. Just glared right at me, standin' in the road like he didn't care if I hit him or not. Either that, or he knew I wouldn't. I swerved around the son of a bitch, called it right in," Filch says. "Let me tell you, that guy spooked me."

Harper scribbles notes on her notepad as he speaks. "That's great. Did you see anything else that might've alerted you to him being up to no good out there? Apart from the fact he was naked, of course . . . and the blood."

"No. Nothin'. I passed his car, a 1988 Chevy truck. I gave the description when I called."

Harper leafs through her notes. "I have it. Anything else about it that you can recall? Any bumper stickers you could see, things like that?"

"Nothing specific. Just one of those trucks you see here and there. No bumper stickers."

"No plate?"

"Sorry."

"That's alright. You've already given us a lot."

Filch nods. "So what is it anyway? A murder or somethin'?"

"Yes and no," Albie says. "We can't really go into detail right now. And we'd ask you to keep this to yourself for the time being."

"Of course. To be honest, I don't even know *what* I saw."

"On that note . . ." Harper hits pause on the recorder. She opens the door and waves someone in: a short middle-aged woman with narrow spectacles perched on the bridge of her nose. "This is Norma. She's our sketch artist. D'you think you can work with her to give us an idea of what this guy looked like?"

"Sure. I can give it a try," Filch says, watching as Albie gives Norma his seat. She sets out her things on the table—paper, pencils, charcoal, a tray of pastels.

"Try to recall as much detail as possible," Norma tells him.

"Excuse us," Harper says. "We're gonna step out for a moment while you do that. We'll be right back."

"Sure thing."

Albie follows Harper out and shuts the door behind them.

"What do you think?" he asks her.

8

"Could be a race thing. Given the description, the fact that the victims are black," she suggests.

"You believe that about the KKK?"

"Stranger things have happened," Harper says with a shrug. "It's a stretch, I know, but we should look into it. Specifically, *you* should look into it."

"Great," Albie says, watching the man through the glass.

"Hey, it gives us another avenue to explore, at the very least. Look at all the convicted racists in the local area. See if the murders correlate to them being out and about. See what you can find out about recent KKK activity in the area. White supremacists, that sort of thing."

Albie nods. "Okay. You're the boss woman."

"You're learning fast, my little apprentice." She pauses for a moment. "It's kind of a long shot, but let's put out a description of the car as well. There can't be that many of those old trucks still on the road."

Albie rolls his eyes. Filch waves at them and they return to the interview room. "What've we got?" Harper asks.

She looks at the drawing Norma has made based on the trucker's description of the man. He looks like a ghoul. Long, stringy arms. Slender body. Odd-shaped, irregular eyeholes staring right back at her. Filch hasn't put eyes behind the mask, only darkness. It gives her chills just to look at it—a cold breeze at the back of her neck, traveling all the way down her spine.

When you gaze long into an abyss, the abyss also gazes into you.

As ever, she feels a burning hatred for the one responsible. It's one thing to be passionate about the job—Harper is passionate about seeing justice served. Catching the bad guys and seeing them safely behind bars. The way it's meant to be done. But seeing these girls turn up dead, it makes her feel a different kind of cold inside. It goes beyond hatred to pure loathing.

"Jeez." Albie peers over her shoulder at the drawing. "Looks the part, huh?"

Harper walks through the parking lot, keys in hand, the sun turning the blue sky white with heat. She inhales deeply to clear her lungs and take in the fragrance of the coast. It smells different here, not quite the same as San Francisco. She wonders briefly if it's the climate or the Atlantic Ocean versus the Pacific.

"We've gotta stop meetin' this way," Stu says, headed toward her. "People will talk."

Harper laughs at that. She shouldn't, but there's no helping it. "Let them."

"How'd it go with the witness?"

"Good. We got some useful info. I've told the trucker to keep himself handy. We'll be calling him at some point, I'm sure," she says. "Norma drew this."

Harper hands Stu a photocopy of the picture Nate Filch described for them.

"Christ," he says, handing it back. "Looks like something out of a fucking horror movie. Are you thinking KKK connection?"

"I've got Albie looking into it, yeah. I'm heading over to the medical examiner's office now. They're going to try and ID the girl."

"Right," Stu says. "I questioned the owner of the land. Just as I thought, it went nowhere."

Harper brushes the hair out of her eyes. "You saw the girl earlier."

"Yeah," Stu says, looking down.

She instinctively steps in close, slides a hand inside his suit jacket and around his waist. They lock eyes and for a moment, a heartbeat, it is just the two of them. "You okay?" she asks him.

Stu looks back up. "No, there's something I need to tell you. It's not about the case."

"Go on."

"Karen's been in touch with me. She thinks gettin' partnered with you split us up. She thinks we had an affair."

Harper takes a step back. "Christ . . . did you tell her that wasn't the case?"

"I tried to, but she wasn't having any of it."

"Why?" Harper asks.

Stu looks away, jaw suddenly tight. "'Cause she's a fucking bitch, that's why."

Harper reaches out, turns his face back to her. "Hey. It's gonna be alright."

"Sure about that? Karen just won't give it up. What've I gotta do?"

Harper doesn't say anything.

"I'd better get going . . ." Stu sighs.

Harper nods, tries to say something, but thinks better of it. Stu turns on his heel and heads for the station. Harper watches him go, a sudden tightening in her chest at the way they've parted—she hates leaving things unsaid.

Stu turns around at the last second and makes the *phone me* sign.

Harper manages a smile, returns the gesture, then goes to her car.

Dead girls wait for no one.

2

Hope's Peak is a modest tourist town on the coast of North Carolina. It has its bay, its beaches. The tourist shops line their pockets in the summer months, then take what they can get when winter hits. Boats run out of the dock every hour—fishing trips, tours of the coastline, diving charters, even a glass-bottomed boat when the weather is good and the sea is calm.

More inland, Hope's Peak is quaint, old-school. Life there appears to be lazy, laid-back, each day passing by in a haze of "who gives a fuck?" whimsy. The town becomes more condensed, more congested before it gives way to endless field and pastures. Miles of green and yellow. Corn crops and soybeans and all manner of things. There are a few parishes that have prospered quietly at the edges of Hope's Peak, but they get little of its trade.

The visitors bring the money. Their money pays for the trash to get picked up, for the hedges to be trimmed. They pay the salaries of the council members.

They are important—they are a bloodline.

◆ ◆ ◆

Harper is left with her own thoughts for company, navigating the afternoon traffic, the air conditioner keeping the inside of the car ice-cold compared to the sticky heat outside.

Six months after Harper arrived in Hope's Peak, she got partnered with Stu Raley. Around the same time, his marriage came to an end. Nearly a year later, she and Stu went for drinks after work, and one thing led to another. There'd been no subterfuge, no affair, but Stu's psycho ex-wife doesn't see it like that.

Harper thinks back to leaving San Francisco, getting as far away as she could, a failed marriage in her wake. North Carolina seemed as good a choice as any. Hope's Peak had charm and character, a world apart from the busy city streets she'd been accustomed to.

The day after she'd slept with Stu the first time, he tried to convince her they couldn't continue with it, that it shouldn't have happened in the first place. Harper shut him up, pressing her mouth against his. When she'd pulled away, she told him that it didn't need to be complicated. They'd both served their time in failed relationships. For the first time in ages, she didn't want to have to feel something. The breakdown of her own marriage back in San Francisco—the way it ended—had left her feeling cold toward anything approaching an emotional involvement.

She'd told Stu it wasn't selfish to want something just for the enjoyment of it. They didn't have to feel guilty or bring anything heavy to the proceedings.

From day one, Stu said how paranoid Karen had been throughout their marriage—now Harper sees it for herself. Stu's ex-wife is imagining something that simply hadn't happened. At least, not the way she thinks—and what Karen is imagining is in danger of becoming an unsettling obsession.

Harper parks outside the medical examiner's office and cuts the engine. She gets out of the car, removes her shades, thinking it wasn't so long ago she attended the autopsy of nineteen-year-old Magnolia Remy.

Found in much the same fashion as that morning's cadaver—raped and strangled. Magnolia's body had been left in a woodland, bloated and covered in bugs by the time they found her.

It was no easy feat, making it through the whole examination, but Harper did it. Dead bodies rarely bother her—it's their ghosts that cause the trouble.

Harper walks into the medical examiner's office, knowing what she will be told. This girl is number two—she hopes she can break the case before the killer claims a third.

A body looks different under fluorescent strip lighting.

The harsh illumination finds every dimple, presents the face as anything but a bland landscape of little feature. Everything looks gray, as if being dead robs you of an essential, humanizing dimension.

Mike and his assistant, Kara, have already been at work on the girl—she has a standard Y incision across the front and down the center of her torso from their investigations. Mike talks Kara through the autopsy while his mic records everything.

"I would posit her age to be mid to late teens," he says.

"Have you run prints?" Harper asks.

"Yes. Nothing on file. Not that I expected there'd be."

"No, of course."

"The victim was hit in the head. There is bruising to her temple, and her jaw." Mike points to the purple marks on the girl's neck. "And strangled to death, as we thought. He applied pressure to her throat until she asphyxiated."

"Poor girl," Kara says.

"No damage to the mouth. I sent over an X-ray of her teeth. Your people are running the dental records now."

Even dental records can be hit-and-miss—if a victim doesn't go to the dentist, there's no record to be checked against. Harper has the same situation with the killer's DNA. She has plenty of it to pin someone to the murder scene, but without that DNA being in the CODIS, it's as useful as teeth no dentist has ever seen before.

The sheet covering the body is pulled down to her abdomen. As clinically detached as Mike can be sometimes, he has respect for the bodies he's presented with. "As we saw previously," he says, careful in his phrasing, "the killer was not kind when he raped her. There is significant tearing, and evidence of internal bleeding."

Harper shakes her head. "Awful."

What this girl went through . . .

"There was some tissue beneath her fingernails," Mike says, lifting the young woman's hand to show Harper. "I've scraped it out and sent it over."

"It'll match what we have already from his semen, but that doesn't do us any good until we have him in custody," Harper says. "No other significant details?"

Mike shakes his head. "Sorry. The toxicology report is fast-tracked, but it won't come back until tomorrow at the earliest."

"What do you expect it to say?" Harper asks him.

Mike turns the victim's head to one side, revealing the puncture mark on her neck. "Dextromethorphan, like the last one. Seems to be his knockout drug of choice. Especially when you consider this girl scratched him in her final moments. You have to be somewhat aware of what's happening when you do that. Maybe he wants them like that."

He steps back and Kara covers the girl over with the sheet. The victim slides back into cold storage with awful finality.

Harper winces at the sound. "Anything else, Mike?"

The ME removes his gloves. "Right now, all we've got is a killer with an inclination toward raping young black girls. He likes to drug them, so we know he prepares ahead of time. That's not passion. That's planning. He hasn't been caught yet, which means either he is very meticulous, or very lucky."

"Sounds on point to me," Harper says. "Samples of hair and everything?"

"CSU finished at the scene. You should get their report by this evening, if they pull their thumbs out of their asses."

"Doubt they'll find anything," Harper says.

Mike shakes his head. "This young woman was just like the last. Killed right where he left her. There was no transportation of the body that I can tell. Once he killed her, he left her where she was. So he transported her while drugged."

"Otherwise we have to ask ourselves what the hell this girl was doing out in a cornfield in the middle of the night . . . okay, thanks Mike."

Harper steps back out into the sunshine. Her stomach rumbles. She should grab some lunch, but there's something about a dead girl in cold storage that makes the thought of a chilled sandwich not so appealing.

She returns to the station and, of course, Mike is right—nothing from CSU to write home about.

John Dudley drops by her desk. "Dental records the ME sent over match those of a girl, east side of the Hill."

He hands her a printout. Harper reads from it. "Alma Buford."

"That's her," Dudley says. "I asked Albie to contact the parents. Do you want to bring them in here or do the interview at their place?"

"Here. Are you okay picking them up?"

Dudley almost grimaces. "Yeah," he says with obvious displeasure.

"Okay," Harper tells him. "Use tact when you break the news to them. It's going to hit them hard."

"Tact is my middle name," Dudley says, walking off before she can say anything else.

An hour later, Art Buford's eyes are shot through with red. His wife, Didi, holds his hand, rubbing back and forth with her thumb. Using her other hand, she dabs at the corners of her eyes with a handkerchief, soaking up the tears that spill out.

This time, Harper is alone. She convinced Stu and Albie that there was no need for them to join her, that having the two of them throwing questions at Alma's parents might be overkill.

"We thought maybe she stayed at a friend's," Didi says, her voice cracking with emotion. "If she didn't turn up by midday, I was going to call the police."

"Lately, we've had some problems with Alma . . . ," Art says. He looks sidelong at his wife, who gives him a nod of the head to go on. "Drinking and such with her friends. You think that might be something to do with it?"

"We're not ruling anything out," Harper says. It's one more thing for her to look into. "You could both try to think of some names for us. Friends she spoke about, who she hung around with . . . any feuds or fallings out. Anyone who might hold a grudge. Maybe boys' names that cropped up. It'd be a big help."

Not telling them we are looking for a male killer, but seeing what they can remember that might point us in the right direction. Did the killer know Alma? Or was she selected the way a hunter tracks deer and chooses one to meet its maker?

Didi starts to sob. "She was such a good girl. I know we had problems lately, but apart from that, she stuck to her books, kept her head down . . ."

"Come here," Art says, putting an arm around her as she holds the hankie to her face.

Harper pushes a box of Kleenex across the table toward Didi. "There's some more in there. Okay?"

"Thanks," Didi manages.

"I want you both to know that we're not taking your daughter's death lightly. We will explore every avenue available to us, anything that will offer insight as to why she died."

"The detective said she was found dead, that she'd been laid out . . ."

"Mister Buford . . . your daughter was murdered. We *are* looking for a killer."

Didi shakes her head, trembling all over. *"Murdered . . . ,"* she whispers in a thin, reedy voice. Her husband holds Didi against his side as she sobs, burying her face in the plaid material of his shirt.

"I'm so sorry," Harper says. This is not the first time she has had to do this. If she can't catch a break in the case soon, she knows it won't be the last either.

Art fixes her with a cold look. *"Find him,"* he growls. "Find whoever killed my daughter."

Before she can catch herself, Harper says, "I will."

Captain Morelli unwraps a hard candy and pops it into his mouth. The sun is sinking outside, casting all of Hope's Peak in deep shadows. Orange light cuts through the blinds in Morelli's office, throwing itself at the back wall in thick contrasting bars of brightness and shadow.

"What do we know about our victim?" Morelli asks Harper.

"Alma Buford. Seventeen. Raped and strangled. Semen matches what we have on record already. Samples taken from under Alma's fingernails also match. It's the same guy."

Morelli sucks the candy. "Right."

"We're waiting on toxicology, but I suspect it'll come back the same thing. DXM to incapacitate her."

"Okay."

"Sir, this sick bastard *will* strike again. His behavior shows psychopathic traits."

"I know," he says grimly. Harper frowns and watches Morelli pick up a file from his desk. He hands it to her.

"What's this?" Harper asks.

"A case."

"If you didn't notice, I already have a pretty big one on my hands."

"Listen to me for a minute, Detective." Morelli holds her gaze. "Many moons ago, I remember there being a girl found up at Wisher's Pond. Twenty-four years old, I believe. Anyway, everything about that case bears more than a passing resemblance to your two girls."

Harper opens the file. She reads the name at the front: "Ruby Lane?"

"The lead on that case is still around. Lives in a retirement home now, if I've heard right," Morelli says. "Might be worth you going to see him. See what he has to say. If this killer is a psychopath, he had to start somewhere. Could be this case has *historic* implications."

"Okay . . . I'll get on it first thing in the morning. Can't very well go pounding on the doors of a retirement home this late at night," Harper says, miffed.

Morelli stands by the window, framed by the fiery light and thick bars of shadow.

"Be sure you do, Detective."

Stu Raley offers her a cup of coffee in the staff kitchen.

"Not for me," Harper says. "I think I'm gonna go home, put my head down."

She watches as Stu stirs several packets of Sweet'N Low into his coffee, then adds a drop of milk.

"Not a bad idea," he says. "Think I'll do a few more hours, though. See what I can turn up."

Harper hands him the file. "This ought to help."

"What is it?" he asks, opening it.

"The captain gave it to me. It was all a bit . . . odd. You know what I mean?"

Stu shakes his head. "Sorry, but no."

"I don't know how to describe it," Harper says, "just that it was out of the ordinary. He said the murder of Ruby Lane matches the two girls we're investigating. But if that's the case, why not hand me this file when we found Magnolia Remy?"

"Maybe he didn't know about the file's existence, or he was waiting to see if there was a pattern. Jesus, you're really worked up over this, aren't you?"

"I don't mean to be. There's just something off about it, that's all," Harper says. "Could be I'm being paranoid."

Stu sips his coffee. "Sure I can't get you one?"

"No, I'm off." Harper reaches for the file but Stu hangs on to it.

"I'll give it to you tomorrow. Let me read through it while I'm here."

"Okay. If you're sure."

Stu smiles. "I am."

Harper pats him on the arm. "Tomorrow, stud?"

"It's a date."

Morelli walks out of his office as Albie and Dudley exit the elevator accompanying a skinny white punk in a wifebeater, jeans, and black combat boots. Cuffs restrain his hands behind his back. He has two full sleeves of tattoos on his arms—the most prominent being the swastika on his right shoulder.

"What's this?" Morelli asks. Dudley doesn't answer. His face is bright red and he's gritting his teeth. His fingers are white hard on the young man's arm. The kid hasn't stopped running his mouth while the two detectives physically maneuver him down the corridor, past Morelli's office.

"You can't arrest me! What for? I didn't do nothin'," he complains, eyeballing the captain as he does so. "Fuckin' pigs!"

Stu ambles over as Albie and Dudley steer the guy into an interview room, despite his protestations. "Skinhead trash, sir."

"Right."

"We're interviewing a few kids, known to be part of a white supremacist group. Don't know what we'll get out of it," Stu tells him.

Morelli nods. "These little pricks hang themselves sometimes, they're so stupid. It's their breeding, Detective. Or shall I say, their inbreeding."

Stu chuckles a little. "I hear you, sir."

Albie emerges from the interview room, flustered.

Morelli calls him over. "Dudley looks wired up," he says.

"The guy rubbed him the wrong way, sir," Albie says.

Stu frowns. "How so?"

"We were talking to this one, just asking questions, when he starts mouthing off to Dudley. Dudley called him a walking cliché, and he called Dudley a filthy nigger-loving mick. Told him the only reason micks get badges is they're too dumb to get real jobs."

"Christ," Stu says.

Morelli shifts on his feet. "What'd Dudley do then?"

"Didn't get a chance to do anything," Albie explains. "Next thing I know, I'm stopping that guy from throwing a punch with Dudley's name on it. We both got on top of the guy and had to restrain him with the cuffs."

"Well"—Morelli sucks his gums, peering down at the interview room door as if he can see straight through it—"just make sure Dudley doesn't do anything stupid."

"I will, sir," Albie says, glancing at Stu, then heads back to the interview room.

The captain rubs the bridge of his nose and yawns.

"Coffee?" Stu offers.

Morelli looks at him, eyes heavy, and smiles. "You know why I like you, Raley? You're a goddamn mind reader."

3

Chalmer, a small hamlet with a population of 857, lies ten miles south-west of Hope's Peak. It is a quiet place, as featureless as the endless, flat farmlands around it.

Bobby Cresswell's sky-blue Lexus has seen better days. It's got a gray fender, and one of the doors has a scratch from top to bottom, now turned a rusted-brown color. The car is all he needs; it runs okay, has never died on him, and goes fast. Nancy Flynn has a way of sitting in the passenger seat, window down, shades on, letting the air whip her hair back as if she's a starlet in an old Hollywood picture. Red Hot Chili Peppers thunder from the stereo, and Bobby beats one hand against the top of the steering wheel, singing along.

He slows at the next turn, a dirt road that leads to a house that has also seen better days—paint flaking off the boards, roof looking like it's about to either cave in or go flying off with the next strong breeze. It stands solitary against the rolling white clouds on the horizon. Bobby turns the stereo down as they approach, the wheels of the Lexus crunching on the hard dirt as he comes to a stop.

"You sure this is the place?" he asks Nancy as they get out.

"That's what Nana said. Right here."

The screen door squeaks on its hinges and a black woman appears on the porch, a white dish towel over her shoulder. She looks to be pushing forty. Her short hair is more gray than black, and she has a cigarette hanging from the corner of her mouth, trailing smoke behind her as she steps out. "Can I help you?"

"I'm Nancy Flynn. This is my fiancé, Bobby Cresswell."

The woman tips her head. "Good to meet you both."

Nancy strokes the swell of her stomach. "My nana said I should come out here and see you."

"Name's Ida," the woman says, her gaze moving to Nancy's bump. "How far along are you?"

"Seven months."

"Your nana wouldn't be Katie Flynn, would she?"

Nancy nods. "That's her."

"Damn. I knew Katie when I was a little girl," Ida says, her face suddenly becoming taut. "You'd better come in. I know what you're here for."

"Thank you," Nancy says.

Bobby begins to follow her in. Ida wags a finger at him. "You wait here, mind your car. Make sure it don't end up with another dent."

Ida leads the way in. Nancy turns to Bobby and shrugs: *What do you want me to do about it?*

The house is tidy but old-fashioned. It smells of cigarettes. That, and something sweet. An old TV is on, the volume down low.

"Are you baking?"

"Bread," Ida says simply. She gestures toward two armchairs. "Sit."

Nancy does as she's told. Ida sits opposite, but not before dragging the chair right in close.

"Now, your nana told you what to bring?"

Nancy digs into her bag and produces two twenties and a ten. She hands the bills over. Ida gives them a cursory look and sets them down on the coffee table.

"Let me see your stomach," Ida tells her.

She lifts her shirt. Ida places both hands on Nancy's bump, the palms of her hands unexpectedly warm. The woman closes her eyes, as if she's listening for something only she can hear. The room grows just a bit darker as the picture on the television fades, then comes back. The volume does the same. Nancy does her best to stay perfectly still. Eventually, Ida's eyes open.

"Boy."

Nancy can't help but be shocked. "Like that?"

The woman picks up the bills and fetches an empty jar from the top of a cabinet. She unscrews the lid, deposits the fifty dollars inside, and screws it shut. "If I'm wrong, you come back here in two months and get that fifty back."

"Okay . . . ," Nancy says, miffed.

Ida disappears into the kitchen, returning with something oblong, wrapped in red-and-white checked muslin, held together with white string. When she hands it over, Nancy realizes it's bread, still warm from the oven.

"Is this for me?"

Ida smiles. It looks weird on her face, as if it doesn't belong there. "No. Your nana."

The Hope and Ruin Coffee Bar on Turner Street is almost empty, though it's not unusual to see cops in there so early, going over one case or another. Harper sips her latte and listens to Stu Raley explain his findings.

"Ruby Lane. Same MO as our two girls."

The photographs attached to the file show her covered in evening frost. In the back of the folder with Harper's notes is a newspaper clipping:

"SNOW ANGEL" MURDER STILL UNRE- SOLVED—HOPE'S PEAK PD STUMPED

"It fits the profile like Morelli said?"

Stu nods. "Trauma to the head and face. The position of the body on the ground matches that of Magnolia Remy and Alma Buford. Could be Ruby Lane's the template for the others."

"Killing them because they're similar to her," Harper says, nodding slowly.

"She was his first kill . . . and she was special."

"Hmm." Harper lifts the folder and leafs through the files inside. "Says here she was living in Chalmer, just her and her daughter. No family, other than her mother and father. It's got interview transcripts with them in here. Her kid must've gone to them when Ruby died."

"Might be worth checking in with them. Track them down, see what they can remember," Stu suggests. "The records at the station got a bit vague at that part, but I did a printout of what I could find."

Inside his notebook, he has several pages he hands to her.

Any record from 1995 onward has been computerized—hence the thousands of files stored in the basement. They could be digitized and disposed of, but that would take time and money the department doesn't have.

Harper reads through what he's given her. "Says here Ruby's mother died in ninety-eight, of natural causes. Ruby's father passed ten years earlier. Suicide."

She goes back a page and follows the third name associated with Ruby: Ida Lane, born 1976. Harper does the mental arithmetic, making

Ida nine years old when Ruby was killed. She works back. Ruby was twenty-four when she died, so she was just fifteen when Ida was born. At first, it's surprising to Harper that Ruby lived away from her parents, since most teen mothers would prefer to stay close to home. And there is no evidence of the father being involved.

She was just a single mom trying to do the right thing.

Harper flicks through the pages until she reaches the point in Detective Lloyd Claymore's notes where he mentions Ruby's daily life. She worked school hours at a dry cleaner's in Chalmer, renting a one bedroom at the back of a bar.

Working, making sure Ida attended school, doing what she could.

Returning to Ida's file, she sees there's not much more. Following the death of her mother, Ida's residence changed to that of her guardians—her grandparents. From the looks of things, unless the records are severely out of date, Ida lives there still. Harper looks at the name adorning each report.

"Detective Lloyd Claymore?"

Stu consults his notes. "Claymore now resides at Baxter Retirement Home, north of Hope's Peak. I've got the address right here."

Harper gets up, takes her keys and bag. "Let's go see what he remembers."

"What about my coffee? I didn't even touch it!"

Harper holds the door open for him. "Ask 'em for a cup with a lid."

Driving through Hope's Peak, Harper calls Albie Goode's phone.

"Albie."

"It's Harper. I'm heading out with Raley, following up on a potential lead. Do you think you could ask around, see what you can turn up about Alma Buford's friends?"

"Sure."

"Thanks. Let me know what you find out."

"Will do," he says.

Harper hangs up.

Stu offers her a stick of gum. "Here."

"Thanks," she says. "Are you saying I've got coffee breath?"

"Nope. And anyway, if *you* do, *I* do, too." Stu pockets the gum. They stop at a set of lights. "Hey, uh, I'll have a talk with Karen. You know, when I've got a chance. Convince her she's wrong about us. She must've heard something from someone."

"How do you mean?" Harper asks.

"Someone's told her we're sleeping together, and that it dates back to before we were divorced."

The lights change. Harper presses the gas pedal and moves with the flow of traffic.

"Who'd do that?" she asks. "We're on good terms with most of the station."

Stu shrugs. "Could be anyone. People gossip too much. You know what it's like in a workplace, how quickly these fucking rumors spread."

Truth be told, they haven't had sex for weeks. With both of them coming out of long-term relationships, the last thing they wanted to do was throw themselves at each other. That, and they'd have to stop working together. Likely she'd get stuck with John Dudley as her new partner.

That is not an option.

"I'm not going to think about it right now, Stu," Harper admits. "There's just the case. Everything else can wait."

"I hear you," he says, knowing all too well why she hasn't been interested in sleeping with him. Since getting assigned to run the Alma Buford case, Harper cannot switch off, and her romantic entanglements with Stu Raley are at the bottom of her list.

They drive on in silence for a while and Harper wonders if what she really meant was that *they* could wait.

She suspects that Stu is wondering the same thing.

The desk clerk at the Baxter Retirement Home calls for a nurse to take them through the east wing of the building. They go through one set of security doors, accessed by punching in a code. There is a short hall, with a few doors on either side, then another security door that prevents any further progress.

"What is this place? Fort Knox?" Stu asks.

The nurse chuckles. "Something like that. We have to be careful. The old folks like to go off and wander."

"*Escape* you mean," Stu says.

"We're extra vigilant today because we lost a resident a few days ago. Most of the staff have gone to the funeral, so we're running a skeleton crew until they come back."

"That's sad," Harper says. "How old?"

"Eighty-six years old," the nurse says. "Went in her sleep."

Stu sighs. "What a way to go . . ."

Harper knows her partner is thinking about those girls, and how they were not afforded the luxury of passing away as they slept.

They're led to a communal area where a few of the residents are playing checkers. One particularly miserable-looking man sits in an armchair, head resting on his chest, snoring, dribble running from his mouth and down his top.

"Don't mind Frank," the nurse says. "That's how he sleeps. It's because he takes his teeth out."

In the corner an old man listens to the radio, head cocked to one side.

"Lloyd—" the nurse starts to say.

The old man waves a hand at him. "Shush for a minute."

Their chaperone shares a look with them. "*Lloyd*, you've got visitors."

Lloyd ignores him.

Harper realizes the old man's listening to the ninth inning of a baseball game. In his hand, he holds a piece of paper, a betting slip.

"You bet the game," Harper says.

Lloyd looks at her, then returns to the radio. "Figure that out all by yourself?"

"I did, actually."

Stu raises a hand in the air. "With my help."

The nurse tells them to take a seat and lowers his voice to a near whisper. "You won't get much out of him till this game is over. Might as well sit down and get comfortable."

As it is, the game only goes on for another few minutes, thanks to a lucky catch turned into a double play by a rookie first baseman, and Lloyd is finished with it. He wads the betting slip up into a little ball and chucks it on the floor. Now he looks at the two detectives with a face that belies his frustration.

"Who're you two?"

"I am Detective Jane Harper. This is my partner, Detective Stu Raley."

"From Hope's Peak PD?"

"Yes sir," Stu says.

Lloyd sits back, hands locked together over his paunch. "Still a shit hole of a place to work?"

"It can be, sometimes," Harper admits. "But that's not why we're here."

"Well whatever it is, don't bother asking me for betting tips. Ain't had a lucky streak for quite some time," Lloyd tells them.

Harper looks at him. Hair almost gone, and what there is of it is pure white. His hands are smothered in age spots. Lloyd's face is deeply lined, his jowls sagging with the years, but his eyes are bright.

"We're not here for tips, Mister Claymore," Stu says. "We're here for help."

"Eh?"

Harper sits forward. "Do you remember Ruby Lane, Detective?"

Recognition flashes. "I do. And it's not 'Detective' anymore. Just Lloyd."

"Okay, Lloyd. Tell us what you remember about her," Harper says.

What he has to say is very much in line with what she's already read from the file, with just a few of the details fudged. Despite that, his memory is remarkably sharp for someone pushing eighty. He recalls names, dates, places. Who said what and where. Harper is impressed.

"You've got a good memory," Stu says.

"Just 'cause I'm in here don't mean I'm senile, son," Lloyd says. He taps the left side of his chest. "It's my ticker's the problem. Not my head."

Stu smirks. "Got it."

"So, her daughter. Ida—"

"Look, if you're here to talk to me about Ruby Lane, that means one thing. That means you've connected some dots. You have a dead girl on your hands. Maybe a few?"

Harper holds up her fingers. "Two."

"And you've noticed a distinct similarity with the murder of Ruby Lane and the two new ones, yes?"

She nods.

"Good. Then it means I can impart something to you both that might be a little . . . sensitive."

"What do you mean?"

Lloyd sighs. He looks at them both. "I've got the cancer. It's in my bladder; it's in my spine. I'm pretty sure it's in my lungs and God knows where else by now. They say I've got six months . . . Well, who knows, eh?"

"I'm sorry to hear that," Stu says.

"While I thank you for your sympathy, it's misplaced, believe me."

Harper cocks her head to one side. "How so?"

"I've kept a secret, Detective Harper. One that has tainted this town long enough. Unfortunately, it's a secret I cannot carry with me to the grave. Not if he's killing again."

"You know who is killing these young women?" Harper asks, sitting forward.

Lloyd shakes his head. "No. But I know there have been others. A great many others, in fact."

"Tell me," Harper says, feeling cold, as if from a draft.

Lloyd is hesitant at first, looking away from them. Harper can see the wheels turning in his old head, deciding whether or not to trust them.

"You can tell me whatever it is you have to tell me," Harper assures him. "I don't have ulterior motives. I'm trying to catch a killer."

Stu clears his throat.

Harper looks back at him. *"We,"* she says with a shake of her head. "We are trying to catch a killer here. Anything you can tell me will help. Anything at all."

Lloyd's tired eyes study her face for a long moment, as if trying to determine the integrity of her character. "I've lived in this town my whole life. Do you understand that? Spending so long in one goddamn place?"

"I guess so . . ."

"Hope's Peak relies on tourist dollars, Detective. The economic fallout if our town no longer had a steady stream of summer vacationers would be devastating. We do well because this is seen to be a respectable place. A little slice of small-town America that people find quaint, charming . . . irresistible, you might say."

Stu says: "I don't get where you're going with this."

"What I'm trying to say is that sometimes good people do bad things because they think it serves a greater purpose. Such as saving a town from ruin," Lloyd says. "Not long after the murder of Ruby Lane, there was another. We'd already received a fair amount of media

34

attention. Before I could attend the crime scene I was called to a meeting. Vince Brookstein, my captain at the time, was there, along with the mayor of Hope's Peak and a number of other people."

"How come there's no record of another murder?"

"I was told in no uncertain terms that if I were to report the murders as what they were, my life would be made very difficult. They made the same case to me as I just did to you. That it would cause irreparable damage to Hope's Peak and the people who live here."

"Disgraceful," Harper says.

Lloyd holds his hands up. "I know, okay? But that's how it was. I concealed evidence so that they could never be connected. I was given strict orders to mislead the public and even some of my colleagues. We made the murders look like accidents, death by misadventure, that kind of thing. You have to understand, these are powerful men, with a lot of similarly powerful men in their pockets. For a long time they have influenced the police, the town council. However, I continued to investigate the deaths on the quiet, in the hope I might find the man responsible but, ultimately, my every effort proved futile. I mean, it's not like I had the assistance of the department, is it?"

"You investigated knowing you couldn't make an arrest," Harper says, shaking her head.

"Who said anything about arresting him? He wouldn't have lived long in my custody, believe me. I knew from the start that there would be no justice sought in his capture. No restitution in his imprisonment," Lloyd says. "Anyhow, for what it's worth, I never managed to make much progress. And every so often a body would turn up. When I retired, someone else took over. Every captain who comes in is sworn to secrecy."

"I don't believe it," Stu says.

"Know what? I don't give half a shit if you believe me. Who's the captain these days?"

"Morelli."

"He told you to come speak to me, didn't he? Told you all about the Ruby Lane case?"

Harper realizes what he is saying. "He set us on our way. I get it."

"The files I kept over the years are in the basement at the station. They've always been there. My altered records, the reports I made up, are in your database, I expect. Go back to Morelli, tell him you want to see the files. He'll know what to do."

Stu stands suddenly. "Call yourself a cop?" he spits, stalking off.

Harper stays where she is. "You telling us this because you think it gives you some kind of . . . redemption?"

Lloyd shakes his head. "No. I'm telling you this because you need to put an end to this legacy. You need to catch this man. And when you do, put a bullet in his head."

"And Ida?"

Lloyd shakes his head, eyes heavy with shadow. "That poor girl."

"She went to stay with Ruby's parents, correct?"

"But it wasn't the end, if you get my drift."

Harper frowns. "I'm afraid I don't."

Lloyd sighs. "Seems that she was let in to see her mother in the casket. You know, the way they do sometimes. All laid out, hair done, dressed in her best clothes, looking like a sleeping angel. In fact that's what they called her, in the papers. Snow angel or some such. When we found her, she was covered in frost, head to toe. Anyhow, I dropped by that day to the chapel. You know, to pay my respects. Broke me, not being able to solve her murder."

"I'm sure seeing Ruby like that did have a lasting effect on Ida."

He shakes his head. "That's not it. She went in there, and from what I heard she reached inside the casket and laid her hand on her mother's. Next thing anyone knew, she was on the floor, out cold. When she woke up . . . well, she wasn't the same. It was like someone took that sweet little girl and wrung her out."

Harper frowns. "What do you mean?"

Lloyd smiles weakly. "Listen, young lady, maybe it's best you go out there, see for yourself. She probably still lives at her grandparents' place."

"I might just do that," Harper says, already dismissing the notion in her head.

She starts to stand. Lloyd slaps a hand on her wrist, holding her in place. The old man looks her right in the eyes and she sees in his, not a retiree, but a fiery detective at his peak. A good man who tried his best but failed.

"Do it," he tells her. "Go see her. She knows something about her mother's death. I always said that girl was the key to solving the murder, but my hands were tied, her being so young and all. She might talk now, if you're lucky."

His hand relaxes around her wrist. Harper gets up.

"I'll drop by her place tomorrow, after I've had a chance to review your old files."

"Good," Lloyd says.

She leaves, pausing halfway across the room to look back at Lloyd. His head is turned away from her, looking out the window. In the reflection in the glass Harper can see him squinting against the sunlight.

Revisiting the past.

"Hey," she says, loud enough to get his attention.

Lloyd looks around.

"I'll drop by again," Harper says. "Let you know if I catch the bastard."

He nods. "You know where I'll be."

Ida sits out on the porch as the sun lifts into the soft white clouds. She'd spent her earliest years in Chalmer before inheriting her grandmother's place outside of town. It did her good to be away from people, from the press of bodies, the rubbing irritation of minds. Out here, on her own, she found peace.

She sips beer straight from the icy-cold bottle, wiping her mouth on the back of her hand. Sometimes she reads, or plays records—old stuff, on vinyl—and just watches the days go by. The world is a great canvas around her, the paint changing by subtle degrees on a daily basis.

Occasionally, she will head into town in her pickup for stores and supplies. There are a few people she will speak to. But for the most part, Ida Lane is a faceless being. A loner black woman living out in the sticks, seemingly content with her own company.

Sometimes it's as if the house in which she spends her days is an axle, and the world turns around it. At night, this far out from the town's illumination, she can see the stars in all their glory, their cold, hard light surrendered to the void. Sometimes it feels like there's a great song she's been listening for, all these years, barely audible at the edge of her hearing.

She lifts the beer and drains the bottle. Despite her taste for suds, she's kept lean. She knows the smokes are a killer, but they're her one true vice.

She thinks, *Everyone's got a vice.*

Ida stretches and heads inside to fetch another beer. She has the thirst like always, and the day is hot.

"Hey hey hey," Albie says as Harper plunks her bag down on her desk. "Lookin' mighty fresh there, Harper."

She throws him a look. "Sucking up to me will get you *everywhere.*"

"He knows it, too," Stu says, patting their young apprentice on the back.

Albie turns to him, looks Stu up and down. "And might I say *you're* looking pretty fine yourself, *Mister Raley!*"

A few of the men working at their desks look up at the sudden increase in volume of Albie's voice. The blood rushes to Stu's head and he removes his hand from Albie's shoulder. Harper can't help but chuckle at the way her partner is instantly uncomfortable around Albie when he does things like that—which, of course, is why he does it.

"I'll, uh, go make some coffee," Stu mumbles, excusing himself.

Harper looks over the scattered contents of her desk, lifting one file, dropping another on top of it. "That's very naughty of you, Albie. You realize you're practically the opposite of what your surname would suggest, right?"

"How can you say that?" Albie grins. "Goode by name, good by nature."

"You wish . . . So where we at?"

"I've got a list of supremacists who were active up to five years ago," Albie says, handing her a printout.

Harper scans the list. "These guys do time?"

"All of them. Aggravated assault, violence with intent, you name it."

Harper nods. "Right. So just the kind of guys you wanna take home and introduce to mama."

"Exactly."

"Well, start looking into them. Each name on the list, in turn," Harper says, handing back the printout. She looks at Albie's face, and there's something amiss. He's about to deliver bad news—she can feel it. "What?"

"Well, you see, John Dudley booked most of these guys before he transferred over. That's what made his name, so to speak. My best bet in getting this done quickly and efficiently is to enlist his help, but I wanted to check with you first. I know you're not exactly simpatico."

Harper sits on the edge of her desk, folds her arms. "Ask Dudley for assistance. Say that I told you to ask for his help, given his history with the KKK."

"You think he'll help?"

Harper shrugs. "If he won't, then I'll talk to him myself. If that fails, I can go to Morelli, but it's best if that doesn't have to happen. Dudley can be asinine if he's not on our side."

"Got it, boss," Albie says, heading off.

Stu arrives at the desk, toting two cups of coffee from the kitchen. "Here you are."

"Thanks, stud," Harper says.

"I bumped into Kapersky. Her toxicology came back," Stu says.

Harper's eyebrows rise. "Yeah?"

"Guess what it was he injected her with . . ."

Harper sighs. "Our old friend, dextromethorphan."

"Exactly."

"I sent Albie off to ask Dudley for help."

"Jeez, is there no other option?" Stu blows across his coffee, then takes a tentative sip. "Damn that's hot . . ."

"Dudley got this far by busting the nutcases posing as the KKK. It's his area. We'd be foolish not to get his help, much as I hate asking."

Stu sighs. "Fuckin' hurts."

Harper looks across to the captain's office. She realizes it's no good putting any of it off. Best to just confront him, see if she can get to the truth.

"You goin' in there?"

She nods.

"Want me to come, kiddo?" he asks.

Harper stands, straightening her shirt. "Nope. You can go check in with Albie, see how he's making out with Dudley."

Stu sags. "Can't we swap?"

Harper is already walking away.

She drops the Ruby Lane file on the captain's desk.

Morelli sits back in his chair, his hands on his stomach. "Hit me with it, Detective."

Harper takes a deep breath. "Captain, I think it's time you told me about the Lloyd Claymore files."

Silence drags out as he considers; then he says: "I need to know I can trust you."

"Of course, sir."

He picks his words carefully, as if he's tiptoeing around a land mine.

"When I was handed this position, my predecessor told me about a series of murders that took place over the years."

"Claymore alluded to them . . ."

"What did he say?"

"He said you'd tell me the truth," Harper says.

Morelli sighs. "Me and Claymore go way back. I was his partner, a couple of years before he retired. Never said a word about any of this. It was only when I got this job that I was let in on our department's dirty little secret."

He reaches inside his desk drawer and hands her something.

Harper looks at it—a small brass key. "I don't get it."

"That's the key to a legacy, and it's high time that it was brought out in the open. When I took this office, my predecessor told me about a locked filing cabinet downstairs. It's the only one down in the basement no one has access to. In there, you'll find everything you need. You have to understand, Detective, that I was told in no uncertain terms: exposing these murders for what they were could seriously harm the town and everyone in it. Sometimes it's best to leave the past in the past."

"Who told you?"

"These are powerful people, Detective. Old money. They're not going to let the murders of a few black girls get in the way of their own affairs."

"I don't understand. Why didn't you act on what you knew anyway?"

Morelli says, "There were other considerations . . . threats against myself, against my family."

"From the people enabling this cover-up? Why not come forward about what they're doing?"

"Things are a little different out here than they are in San Francisco, Detective."

Harper weighs the key in her hand. "We swore an oath to protect the innocent, to see that justice is served to the full letter of the law . . . and here we are, hiding the truth, holding back the course of justice."

Morelli rubs his tired eyes. "I know these murders will never end. And I can't go on any longer, living with the guilt. The injustice of it all goes against everything I joined law enforcement for. It's time something was done to bring these to light. I'm just sorry it took me this long to find the courage."

"You realize I need to bring Stu Raley in on this?"

"Of course; I trust Raley," Morelli says. "I thought it was all over with. Yet . . . here we are."

"Here we are," Harper repeats, shaking her head with distaste.

"Don't judge me for protecting my family, Detective. If the truth had gotten out, these people might have come after my wife, after my kids. But I can't sit on my hands any longer. It's time I started making things right." Morelli fixes her with a hard glare. "The murders were covered up. Details changed about the circumstances of their deaths. Little things, enough to make them appear to be unconnected. No mention of the crowns he leaves on their heads, for one thing. But now you know the truth. And this is your chance at cracking this case."

Harper gets to her feet, eager to get down in the basement and start digging. "Keep this between you and Raley, okay? At least until the time is right. We don't need media attention drawing our focus away from what's important—finding the sick son of a bitch who's killing these girls. Everything else can be handled after."

"Yes sir," Harper says.

"Right. Don't let me hold you back any further. Let's get out there and catch this bastard," Morelli says, waving her off. He turns to the pile of papers on his desk that awaits his attention. "Good hunting."

As she walks away from his office, Harper can't help but feel a chill run down her spine. There are people with so much influence, with such a stranglehold over the town, that they have kept these murders covered up for so long. To what lengths will they go for what they think is the good of the town?

The basement—or dungeon, as the cops often call it—consists of rows of rolling shelves. By cranking a wheel on the edge of the unit, you move the shelf across, allowing access to its contents. The shelves have laminated printouts on the ends, with the contents of each mobile stack listed alphabetically and by category. On the other side of the basement are rows of old filing cabinets, and down one end is a caged-off area for sensitive evidence. A senior officer holds the key to the evidence lockup, and everyone has to be signed in and out.

"I don't get the subterfuge," Stu says, peering left and right. They're the only ones down there. "I mean, what's it all about, huh?"

"You'll see."

She instructs him to try opening the cabinets. One by one they attempt to yank them open, succeeding every time. Stu arrives at the last cabinet and tries it. It won't budge. "Hey . . . sucker won't open."

"This must be the one."

Harper slides the key into the lock and opens it up. The top and middle drawers are completely empty. Only the bottom holds anything—a dozen or so files, held together like a Christmas present with white twine.

"What's that?" Raley asks.

Harper scoops the files out of the cabinet and kicks the drawer closed with her foot. "This could be our big break. Let's go to my apartment, away from prying eyes. You can drive."

"This is gonna give me a fucking ulcer," Stu complains when they get through the door to her apartment. "This whole case is a nightmare."

Harper sets the files down on her kitchen counter and proceeds to cut the twine with a pair of scissors. She recounts how Captain Morelli handed her the key. "It was like 'and this is your responsibility now,' you know?"

"Damn," Raley says, pulling out a chair from her dining room table and sitting down. "So they're the files Claymore was talking about."

"Yeah. Now remember this has to stay between us, at least until we catch this guy."

"I get that; I'm not dense. Just the two of us." Stu takes a deep breath. "Okay, so where do we begin?"

Harper hands him the file off the top. "We read."

It's late by the time they've read through all the files to establish a broad sweep of events. The files are arranged chronologically.

Ruby Lane, 1985. Followed by Odetta Draw in early 1987. They go on like that, one every couple of years, with a quiet period of five years when there were no mysterious deaths at all . . . until Magnolia Remy and Alma Buford, that is.

Harper rubs her eyes. "Assuming they were all committed by the same guy, that's a total of ten victims."

Black girls. Raped. Strangled. Body fluids left at the scene. Most of them exhibiting other signs of violence, and puncture marks from hypodermic needles—no toxicology reports because, of course, that would arouse suspicion and make the cover-up impossible.

"There's definite evidence of serial activity. The killer does the same thing, over and over. And after what looks like a brief hiatus, he is increasing his activities. Like someone who smokes ten cigarettes a day moving to twenty, then forty . . . the killer's turned it up a notch," Stu says.

The recent bodies—Magnolia Remy, Alma Buford—will cause a stir in the news, of that Harper has no doubt. "Ten girls, and more to come."

"We'll get him."

"Let's hope so." Harper pats the files. They're so much more than sheets of paper. They are an inconvenient truth, each folder detailing the end of a life. "I really don't want to have to add to this pile."

"Me neither. So what's the next play?" Stu asks.

"Cross-reference these with what we have at the station. See if there's anything from these files that's actually helpful. In the meantime, I'll catch up with Albie, see how he's doing with Alma Buford's friends. They might remember something odd going on."

"Right," Stu says, getting up. "I might grab a few files now. Something to read tonight."

She shakes her head. "Hey, Stu? Don't do that. Let's both get a good night's rest and attack it fresh tomorrow, huh?"

"Sure," he says. "You wanna go grab something quick to eat? I feel like I haven't spent a lot of time with you."

Harper looks at her watch. "If you don't mind, I think I'll just have a shower and go to bed. I'm bushed."

"Miss Sensible."

"Ha! I wish."

"You can come stay at my place tonight if you want."

"Thanks, but not tonight. Not with Karen on the warpath," Harper says, seeing the instant disapproval. "I'm in no mood for somebody else's bullshit, you know?"

Not that I give two hoots what she thinks.

"Okay, okay," Stu says and walks to the door. He turns back, hand on the knob. "You won't change your mind?"

She smiles. "Night, Stu."

Two hours later, Harper pads through the apartment fresh from the shower, one big towel wrapped around her body, another containing her wet hair.

In the kitchen, she makes a cup of tea—made the proper way, with leaves, stewed in a good pot—no milk, no sugar. Usually she's a latte girl, but there's something about tea that is so calming. She holds the cup in both hands, sipping it as she looks at the board on the wall—the only bit of decorating she's done in there, screwing the thing to the plaster.

A map shows their little corner of North Carolina. While they were reading the files, Harper scribbled the name of each victim on a scrap of paper. Each red pin stuck into the board holds one of those names.

Over two decades of unsolved murders.

She knows that Morelli is still one of the good guys, or he wouldn't have given her the key. But, had Magnolia Remy and Alma Buford not died, Harper doubts he would have thought to let the truth out. Like his predecessors, he would've let it sit in that filing cabinet, closing his eyes and grateful the responsibility never fell on him to do otherwise. Except, now it had.

Trouble is his hands were dirty before his first day in the office.

When it all comes out, Harper's not so sure Morelli will be able to deny any knowledge of the cover-up. She got his point, though, about protecting the town. The people around Hope's Peak are farmers and planters. Some of them in the fishing industry, but for the most part, their profession involves working the Carolina soil with their own hands. In the town, the trade's whatever blows in on the breeze—the tourists and sightseers who keep Hope's Peak afloat.

It has small-town charm, and plays on that to draw the vacationers looking to catch a break from the city. A serial killer who's gotten away with what he's done for decades wouldn't do much for the town's appeal.

And all the victims—so far—have been local. That's a close call for Hope's Peak. It would take only one outsider getting killed to have the whole situation become a national event.

Harper looks at the map. The red pins are clustered around Hope's Peak and Chalmer just to the southwest.

The killer has to be local.

Harper sips her tea. Her cell phone vibrates. She looks at the caller ID: it's Stu. "Hey," she says, holding it to her ear.

"How're you doing?"

"Oh, just chilling now. Going over today. You know."

"Yeah."

"What about you?"

"Drinking a beer. Trying to get my head around all this. First the body, then these cold cases. A murder and a colossal cover-up in the space of two days. It's been a hell of a week so far, kiddo."

Harper gets closer to the board on her wall and finds the pin holding the first murder: Ruby Lane, found strangled and sexually violated in the tall grass at Wisher's Pond. November 14, 1985.

The next: Odetta Draw, strangled, raped. Body found in a state of decomposition in an abandoned barn outside of Hope's Peak. January 10, 1987.

On and on.

"You listening? You've gone quiet . . ."

"Huh? Oh, sorry! I was looking at my board. I got lost for a second there. What were you saying?"

Stu sighs on the other end. "Never mind. I'll meet you at the station tomorrow. I want to get on those records first thing, let you know what I turn up."

"Okay."

"You keeping the files at your place?"

"For the time being, yeah. But I think we should move them back to that locker. I mean, there's only one key and we have it. No one's going to see them but us."

"Jane, are you alright?" Stu asks her.

"Of course. Night, Stu."

"Night."

Harper puts the phone down and drains the last of her tea. She looks at the files on the table. For a moment, she considers starting again on Ruby Lane, but finds she's too tired to move. She sits back and closes her eyes.

All she can see is the young woman lying in the dirt, and the disjointed shadows from the corn giving the impression of being underwater.

4

A breath of wind and ripples fan out over Wisher's Pond. The woman calls his name, treading through grass tall as her hip. A bird caws somewhere in the trees, which tower starkly against a sky of washed-out nothing. Her voice falters at the sound of someone approaching.

She turns. Her mouth works soundlessly, trying to scream, but there is no breath there, no voice left in her throat but a frightened wheeze. All she can do is stumble back, feeling out for something to steady her, to regain her footing. But there is only the grass, and it welcomes her with its soft embrace . . .

Ida Lane wakes, body wet with sweat, heart driving a heavy percussion in her ears. She sits, wiping away the tears that streak down her cheeks. The house is dark, the air still.

She strips out of her damp pajamas, throwing on every light to every room she passes through as she heads downstairs. She pours herself a glass of milk and switches on the TV. The clock on the wall says it's three in the morning.

She has suffered the same dream since her mother passed those many years ago, and it plays the same way every time, without fail. Her final moments, falling into a mattress of fine grass. There is a blanket on the sofa, and Ida pulls it over her naked form as she shivers at the recollection.

The news comes on and the ticker at the bottom of the screen makes her freeze, every muscle in her body bunched up tight, knotted like a rope under strain. She grips the glass so tight she has to set it down before it smashes apart in her hand.

HOPE'S PEAK GIRL FOUND MURDERED— LOCAL PD SEEKS KILLER

Ida buries her face in her hands. She can't stop the sobs that come— they rise from a spring of cold water deep inside. Ida thinks of their bodies, left out under the starlight, the frost settling on their skin and in their hair. Chilled, as her mother was when they found her.

She often thought of her mother during her four-year stay at Hope's Peak Psychiatric Hospital—her mother's murder plagued her every thought at first. In the day, she would brood, in a fog of medication and therapy. By night, Ida dreaded the shroud of sleep, and the dream that always came with it.

One night she woke, climbed out of bed, and paced her room. It suddenly occurred to her what she must do. Ida walked out to the hall and made her way to the nearest fire escape. She'd often seen the nurses disable the alarm on the door so they could stand there and smoke without having to go all the way out. It was the height of winter, and bitterly cold.

Ida thought: *I will sparkle with starlight.*

The key was still in the alarm panel. She turned it to the "Off" position, shoved the bar on the door. Freezing night air rushed into the hospital as Ida stepped out, hugging her body against the cold, yet welcoming it at the same time. She looked up at the night sky, at the brilliant moon above the hospital roof spilling its pearlescent light on the frozen lawns stretching into the darkness.

By the time the nurses found her, Ida had given herself to the cold night. She'd wanted to join her mother, wanted to shine under the stars. It took a long time to nurse her back to health. After that, her bedroom door stayed locked at night.

Lester Simmons moves the arm and drops the car's hood back into place with a loud bang. He climbs in the driver's side and starts the engine—as expected, it starts first time. Not the choked sputtering sound it had made before, but a steady rumble. He turns the key, silencing the engine of the old Ford Granada. He wipes his oily hands on a rag, stuffs the rag into his pocket, and walks through the garage into the house.

Ceeli is out in her backyard, hanging laundry. She turns around, startled by his sudden appearance at the back door; he's watching her in her faded housedress, the afternoon sun adding a shine to her dark-brown skin. "Jesus, Lester! You nearly gave me a heart attack!" she cries, smiling all the same.

"I fixed the problem," he says. Lester is in his early sixties, with bushy gray hair on either side of his pale-white, bald, domed head. But he's not old—he has long, gangly arms, the tops heavy with muscle. His body is lean. To look at him, it's not hard to imagine Lester has naturally inherent strength. He is the sort of man who can turn a wrench on a bolt no other man can budge, but when he walks, he lumbers at his own pace, as if he hasn't yet learned how to use his gigantic feet.

"Oh good. I did worry about it," Ceeli says. "Now, how much do I owe you?"

He shakes his head. "No charge."

"Come on, Lester. Let me give you something."

"Honeſtly," he says, grinning. His cleft lip lifts to show the gum above his top front teeth. When his mouth is closed, the deformity isn't as noticeable. But smiling, or laughing, Lester assumes a freakish appearance.

He has never said an *S* his entire life.

Ceeli moves close, her hand on his crotch. "Honey, you sure I can't do nothin' for you?"

Lester's eyes stop on her full lips before he looks away. "Not today. Wanna get on my way. Pretty tired."

Dejected, Ceeli removes her hand and goes to the fridge. She removes a six-pack and hands it to him. "At least let me give you these. Mack won't notice. Probably think he drank 'em already."

Lester bows his head in thanks.

Brightening a little, Ceeli smiles at him. "You know, you're a good man, Lester. What would I do without you around?"

He smiles gruesomely. "Well, I better get goin'."

"Sure, honey." Ceeli walks him to the door. At the last moment, she blocks the way out, gets in close to him, her rank breath washing over him as she whispers in his ear. "You come by soon, you hear? I'll call you when Mack's away next."

"Okay."

She grabs his crotch again, this time giving his fruits a firm squeeze. "And keep that big ole tire iron handy." With that she pecks him on the cheek and opens the door.

Lester goes to his truck, a late-eighties model with scuffed gray paint, starts the engine, and looks back at the house. Ceeli waves. "Thanks again!" she shouts across the street.

Lester waves back and peels away from the curb. He heads for home—the house on the outskirts east of Hope's Peak where he has lived his entire life. At an intersection, he stops and waits for the light to change. A bus goes past, deposits several passengers at the stop to his left. An old lady, two young schoolboys, a mother with a baby carriage, and a black girl.

The girl is late teens at least, early twenties at the most, hair braided back in pigtails. Tall, slender, good-looking. Lester feels that all-too-familiar stirring within him. The same tingle you get along your forearms at the sound of a familiar song.

I told you about that girl lester that little bitch is like all them blacks not one of 'em don't deserve what they got comin'. . .

The light changes. The girl walks to the left, out of sight. Lester should turn right and head for home, but he turns left and follows her along the street.

She walks in a daydream, doesn't notice him. The street leads to a road that cuts through the fields, crops on either side. A big red barn on a hill to the right. Lester drops his speed, takes his time. There are no other cars on the road, not in front or behind. He follows her as she walks on her own for a solid twenty minutes before arriving at the gate of a farm. The bus doesn't come out here. Lester speeds up, and she half turns to watch him pass as she opens the gate and continues on toward a big farmhouse at the end of a lane. Lester looks in his rearview mirror at the farm falling away behind him, the girl.

There it is: the same tightening in the chest he gets each time. Something has stirred, touched him in a way Ceeli only wishes she could when her husband, Mack, is working. It's lust, it's the warm, fuzzy glow of attraction all swirled together, like the red-and-white stripes in a lollipop.

Them feelin's you got they ain't real they that ole black magic workin' on ya turnin' your head from what you been taught from how you been raised . . .

Lester finds a place to turn around, the car tires kicking up dust and dirt as he backs up on the grass. He heads back toward the farm and slows to a stop outside it, looking at the house, the chickens milling about the front. Then he gets into gear and speeds off, eager to get home now, feeling newly invigorated.

The way he always does when he falls in love at first sight.

The supplejack vine grows at the edge of an abandoned property a few miles down the road, where the woods start. Lester collects whole lengths of it, snapping them off and holding them in a bunch. He picks them for girth, for uniformity.

Back home, he sits in his shed carefully interlacing the vines, tugging at them to make them hold together, but not so tight that they might snap as they dry. He does so around a broken cookie jar his mama used to keep—it gives the perfect circumference to create a crown.

Decades before, he spent hours weaving such a crown for Ruby Lane. He didn't know what she would think of it, or if she'd understand the hobby of a lonely boy with time on his hands. She put it on and Lester told her how pretty she looked as she circled in front of him, looking every bit the princess he thought her to be . . .

A crow caws outside.

Sweat drips from Lester's nose and hits the vine. He holds it up. The crown is perfect. It might be the best he's done yet. He pictures Ida's mother standing before him once more, the crown on her head; then he pictures it on the new girl. Lester smiles at the thought of how beautiful she will look when the crown—his work—sits atop her head.

Harper pats her pocket for the key to the filing cabinet. She has already stowed the files back in there, then double-checked that it was locked.

But what will I do if I lose the key?

With that thought, Harper takes it out of her pocket, hooks it on to her car keys. She starts the car and lets it run for a moment as she puts her cell in its dock on the dash. Almost immediately, the screen flashes the first few words of a new text message. She swipes the screen. It's from Stu:

```
Call me when U R done today. Let me know
how it goes.—SR
```

Harper smiles, tapping a quick reply onto the phone's on-screen keyboard.

```
Ok. Any developments YOU call ME Btw I
put the files back. I will give you the
key or we can make a copy.
```

The land is flat, brown, and green. Every shade of nature you can imagine, all of it subdued, laid-back. A haze settles permanently upon the horizon. Dust thrown up off the roads looks like muddy smoke.

Harper crosses the railway track that borders Chalmer. An old Dean Martin number comes on the radio: "Powder Your Face with Sunshine."

It makes her think of her childhood, something she'd rather forget. To that end, she switches the radio off and drives the rest of the way in silence. The main street feeds the rest of the little town like a major artery pumping blood to every extremity. Chalmer branches off of Hope's Peak in such a way that Harper finds it hard to understand why it's a separate entity from its bigger counterpart.

She parks outside the sheriff's office.

"Hey," Harper says to the officer at the front counter. She removes her sunglasses and sets them down before producing her ID. "I'm looking for a bit of info on one of your residents."

"That so?"

"Yes. Ida Lane. I think she lives out on the—"

The deputy raises a hand to stop her. "I know Ida. She in trouble or somethin'?"

"No, no. I just want to ask her a few questions relating to a case I'm working."

"Aha. I see. You want something . . . unofficial," he says.

Harper glances left and right—she's the only one in there. "Why the games? Can you tell me something or not?"

"Afraid not."

Harper grabs her glasses, and starts to leave. She gets as far as the door.

"If you want to know about Ida Lane, you need to talk to Hank Partman."

She turns back. "Partman?"

"Outside, turn left. He owns the little store down there, Past Times. Sells collectibles and such. Talk to him," the deputy says, returning to whatever he was writing before she walked in. Harper opens the door and walks out, frowning back into the quiet sheriff's office.

She gets the feeling this is very much one of those towns. Not that there's something fundamentally wrong here—just that it's slightly off-kilter. Like the deputy on the desk.

In her two years living in Hope's Peak, she's never had cause to visit Chalmer, and there's a flavor of the weird that's hard to miss.

Past Times is a dusty place, with a bell on the door, crammed full of merchandise. A withered old man comes out from behind a counter with a cash register on top.

"Afternoon," Hank says, flashing a set of perfectly straight false teeth. "Can I help you with anything?"

She shows him her ID. The smile fades, just a little. "I'm looking for some info."

"Information on what, exactly?"

"On whom. I'm told you're a man in the know when it comes to local matters," Harper says.

Hank Partman leans against the counter, his ego stroked. "I've been known to be quite knowledgeable, yes. To whom are you referring then?"

"Ida Lane?"

"Oh," Partman says, looking down, smile nothing but a distant memory now. "I doubt there's much I'll be able to tell you that you don't already know . . ."

"Really? That's a shame," Harper says, unconvinced. She decides to turn on the charm, put her feminine wiles to good use. "I bet there's quite a bit a man like you could tell me. A respected member of the parish, and all that."

Partman blushes. "Well, of course there was her poor mother's murder . . ."

"Yes."

Partman removes his glasses and uses the end of his tie to clean the lenses. "Then her grandpappy killing himself the way he did," Partman says with a shake of the head.

"How did that happen?"

"Oh, he hung himself. I believe it was poor Ida found him," Partman explains, a distinct note of sadness in his voice. "He was swinging back and forth. She never really stood a chance, poor thing. It's no wonder she's the way she is now."

"Does anyone see much of her?" Harper asks.

"She lives out there in the house she grew up in, right on the edge of Chalmer. Hardly says boo to anyone when she pops into town. Does come in here from time to time, though."

Harper frowns. "Really? What for?"

"This and that. Bought a typewriter off me a few months back. You know, the manual type. She came in last week, got a replacement ribbon for it. Lucky I had some in stock. They're hard to get these days.

I think she likes to live simply. I was surprised to hear she even had a TV. No video, though."

"Friends? Anything like that?"

Partman shakes his head. "Not that I know of. I think Ida's happy living on the outskirts, where it's quiet. She buys a lot of records off me sometimes."

"Records?"

"Vinyl. Twelve inches. Old stuff, you understand."

It never ceases to amaze Harper the little details people remember. "Right. Okay. Thanks."

She starts to leave, and Partman comes out from behind his counter. "Miss Harper?"

"Yes?"

"People around here respect her privacy," he says, his eyes full of sadness. His voice drops to a soft whisper. "I think they pity her . . . and they maybe even fear her. Just a little."

"Fear her?"

"Just a little."

"Why?"

"Ida is different. You'll see when you get up there. It really was tragic, what happened to her. To be honest, I'm a little surprised she hasn't followed in her grandpappy's footsteps by now."

The house could do with a coat of paint. Maybe two.

Harper gets out of the car and immediately sees movement from inside.

A black woman in her late thirties pushes through the screen door and walks out onto the porch. "Hey."

Harper walks to the front steps leading up to the porch. "Hi, I'm Detective Jane Harper. Would you be Ida?"

"I would. Why d'you ask?"

"May I speak with you?" Harper asks.

Ida shrugs. "Sure."

When Harper gets to the porch, however, Ida shows no sign of going back indoors. "Hey, uh, can I see some ID first?"

"Oh, yeah," Harper says, handing it to her.

"Okay." Ida gives it back. "Do you want to sit out here? It's awful hot inside and I don't have a fan since my last one decided to die on me."

"I'm fine either way," Harper says, sensing the woman's initial reluctance to invite a stranger inside. "However you like."

Ida leads her to a swinging chair around the side. The bolts holding it in place look rusted and old, but when Harper sits in it, it's sturdy enough. Ida sits at the other end, pulling a cigarette from a pack.

"Care for one?"

"No thanks. I don't smoke."

Ida shrugs. "Huh. Mind if I do?"

"Go ahead," she says, watching Ida slip the cigarette between her lips, strike a match, and light it.

"So what can I do for you, Detective? I don't get many visitors out here, so there must be some special reason you've made the effort."

Harper clears her throat. "Alma Buford. She was the young woman found murdered two days ago. I'm the lead on the case."

"Alright," Ida says flatly, giving nothing away.

Harper licks her top lip. "I'm looking at the historical murders that we believe are the work of the same individual. I happened upon your mother's case—"

"Look," Ida interrupts her. "I don't really want to go into all that."

"I'm not going to force you to divulge anything you find too traumatic. I just want to see if there's something about Ruby's death that hasn't been explored yet."

Ida shakes her head with disdain. "There ain't nothing that ain't been gone over a thousand times by now. It's in the past. Best leave it there."

"I don't mean to cause offense," Harper says. "I'm just exploring every avenue. I want to stop this guy before he kills another innocent young woman."

Ida stands. "Well *this* particular avenue is well and truly shut. I'm sorry, Detective, but there's nothing I can tell you. Opening old wounds is no good for anybody, especially the kind I got."

"Please, Miss Lane. There might be some small detail that helps us catch this man. Isn't that worth it?"

"Like I said, Detective"—Ida stubs her cigarette out, face tight with tension—"I think you're wasting your time here."

"Well, thank you anyway," Harper says.

She heads for her car and glances back up at the porch. Ida is watching her, an unreadable expression on her face. Harper starts the engine and begins to drive away, not entirely sure what just happened but knowing it does nothing for her case.

When she looks back in the mirror, Ida is still there, watching her.

Ida watches the detective's car kick up a trail of dust in its wake and can't help but feel a pang of regret at the way she responded to her questions.

But it had to be done—she's spent her whole life reliving the past, waking from the same nightmare over and over.

Her grandmother once told her she was *touched* by a wonderful gift, that she was put on this earth to help others.

I was tainted by my ability. If I was destined to do anything, it certainly wasn't to help people. It was to live in misery.

She watches the detective's car merge with the haze on the horizon and remembers finding her grandfather hanging from the rope.

His eyes are wide open, staring straight into her. The rope still creaks—he hasn't been dead for long. Legs completely straight, arms by his sides. Face dark purple, rope cutting in under his chin.

But those eyes!

They bulge from the sockets, bright red, every vein filled with harden-ing blood. Looking right at her, into her, past her. Ida wants to run, wants to scream, but can't. All she can do is watch as he swings, back and forth, back and forth. Only her grandmammy's hand on her shoulder from behind snaps her back. The old woman's wail as she hugs Ida to her and steers her away from him.

He'll always be swinging, just as her mother will forever be fall-ing. The rope will creak in the gray moment between wakefulness and sleep.

Ida snaps to, aware that her cheeks are wet. The memory came back strong—it does sometimes, when she least expects it. She wipes the tears on the back of her hand, goes inside, snatches her keys from the sideboard, and rushes to her truck.

Harper hears the pickup before she sees it. It rushes up from behind, engine roaring, driver waving one brown arm from the open window, signaling for her to pull over. She slows, bringing the car to a halt, the truck doing the same behind her.

She is confident that Ida Lane is not some nutcase, driven mad by misfortune, intent on doing her harm. Still, Harper watches in her side mirror and unclips the top of her holster as Ida gets out of her truck.

Just in case.

She gets out of the car. "I have colleagues who would probably consider that reckless driving."

"Sorry. I needed to get you to stop," Ida says breathlessly. "I was rude back there."

"You were a little abrupt, I'll give you that," Harper says. "Have you had a change of heart?"

Ida looks away. There are endless rows of soybean crops on either side of the road, several feet high. "Have you ever lost someone?" she asks.

The question throws Harper for a second. "Not like you, no."

"I believe we all got ghosts, Detective. People we lost, people we let down. I think I been haunted by mine for too long. I feel their weight, right here round my throat, like my grandfather's rope," Ida says. She looks at her. "If this man is killing these women . . . and if he killed my mother . . . I want to help."

Harper nods. "I'm glad to hear that. Shall we go back to your house and talk?"

"Yeah."

On the drive back to Ida's, the truck now traveling at a relative crawl considering the speed she'd driven at earlier, Harper has time to wonder just what it was that changed Ida's mind.

The inside of the house isn't nearly as hot as Ida said it would be. Harper has a digital recorder on the table between them. Much handier than a notepad and pen, with the added boon that she can play it back through the car stereo. Often, she will leave an interview or meeting and listen back through what's just taken place, in the hope of finding new meaning or insight.

"I know it's hard, but I'd like you to think back to your mother. Did she ever have male friends hanging around? Boyfriends?"

Ida shakes her head. "Not that I remember. There was Daddy, but she never saw him since the day she said she was pregnant. To this day, I ain't met the man. Don't even know his name."

"Can you remember if she ever had friends from work? Anyone she would hang out with?"

"Again, it's all a bit of a blank, I'm afraid."

"Doesn't matter. You can't force these things. They either come or they don't."

Ida lights a cigarette. "I do remember my mother, though," she says, the suggestion of a smile crossing her features. "I think about her all the time."

"What was she like?" Harper asks.

"Very beautiful. No-nonsense hair. Pulled back tight, out of the way 'cause of the heat. Always there for me, always around. She was a good mom."

"I understand."

Ida draws on the cigarette, rolling the milky-blue smoke around before blowing it out the side of her mouth. Lost in thought, lost in memory.

I believe we all got ghosts.

"She was young, but she knew what she was doing. Always did right by me, I remember that," Ida says, smiling now at the memory. "Sometimes at night when I had trouble sleeping, she'd sit on the bed. It'd be dark, maybe just the light from the hall. Made her a silhouette to look at. She'd just sit there and sing in that soft voice of hers. I think sometimes maybe that's what I miss the most, that sweet, sweet singing . . ."

I been haunted by mine for too long.

"You sound like you miss her," Harper says.

"Yes," Ida says without hesitation. "Yes, I do."

"I know it's hard to talk about, but I'd like you to tell me about your mother's death. What do you remember about it? I know you were young at the time."

Ida draws on the cigarette. "Only that she went missing, and was found. And then there was *after*."

"What do you mean?"

"Her funeral."

It's suddenly hotter in the house, and Harper suppresses the urge to pull at her collar or take her suit jacket off. She sits as if nothing has changed, but there's definitely a shift in the air—as if the whole house has tensed in expectation.

"I went to see her. Laid out in the casket. You know something? It happens so fast. You must see it on your end of things. But when you lose someone like that, everything takes on a kind of quickness. There isn't time to catch your breath. One morning your mother's seeing you into school. A day later, she turns up dead. A short while after that, you're visiting her in her coffin, saying good-bye."

Harper expects tears from Ida, but none come. She just sucks on that cigarette, as if drawing strength from it. Clutching the smoke in her lungs for as long as she can, till it burns, then slowly releasing it.

Watching her smoke, Harper begins to see why Ida lives on her own, so far from town. Why she needs space. Harper thinks back to what Lloyd Claymore said: *It was like someone took that sweet little girl and wrung her out.*

Ida takes her time, and Harper lets her. Sometimes the key to a revealing interview is letting the interviewee just talk. Giving them room to breathe and release what's locked up inside.

"I couldn't believe it was her. She looked like she was just asleep. They did a real good job, let me tell you. I thought I could just reach out, touch her, and it'd all be alright. Silly, huh? I put my hand on hers and the first thing that hit me was just how cold she was. Like touching marble. And then it happened."

"It?"

Ida stubs the cigarette out. "Detective, do you think a person can tell what another person is thinking? Like, hear their thoughts?"

"I've heard stories," Harper says. "But I'll admit, I've never really believed that kind of stuff."

Now Ida smiles. "What if I told you that I touched my mother's hand and saw the entire murder? Everything but the killer's face. I dream about it even now. Every night, over and over. There's barely a night goes by I don't wake, soaking wet I'm so scared."

Harper sits forward. "You say you *saw* the entire murder . . ."

"As if I were there. I think afterward, I passed out. It was too much," Ida says. "I guess I got a bit overloaded."

"Are we talking some kind of . . . psychic thing here?" Harper asks. She is wondering how long it will take her to get out of the house without causing offense. Make her excuses to wrap it all up quick and get on the road. Either Claymore was pulling her leg, or he believed such nonsense.

Ida smiles knowingly. "Detective, you don't have to hide your distrust. I don't blame you. Just another crazy black woman living out in the sticks, huh?"

"No, no, no! Not at all!"

Ida sits back, arms folded. "I touched my mother's hand. It felt like an electrical charge, jumping from her to me. And nothing around me mattered anymore because the vision was on me. It felt like a heavy curtain around my shoulder, pressing down on my head. It was this weight. Everything turned black. My grandmammy's voice called for help, but I wasn't there anymore. I was wherever her spirit led me. Another place, away from the light."

"Go on . . . ," Harper tells her in a soft voice. Part of being a good detective is allowing a person time to reveal the truth. Playing along for the sake of furthering the case.

Cop 101 is to never tell the crazy person you can or can't see the dragon. Just tell them you believe they can see it.

Harper looks at Ida and wonders if she knows more than she's letting on. The crazy person routine could be a defense mechanism, Ida's way of coping with her experiences. Not unlike people who report being abducted by UFOs when, in fact, they were molested as a child.

Our bodies have remarkable ways of protecting us from harm, even when that harm is psychological.

"Let me tell you the dream, which was the vision I had. Okay? See what you think."

Ida describes everything to her—how it is in her head, how it plays in her dreams. "There's wind, and it pushes over the pond. You know, the way it does. Making the water ripple, kind of fan out . . ."

Ruby calls his name, treading through grass tall as her hip. A bird caws somewhere in the trees, which crash against a sky of washed-out nothing. Her voice falters at the sound of someone approaching.

She turns. Her mouth works soundlessly, trying to scream, but there is no breath there, no voice left in her throat but a frightened wheeze. All she can do is stumble back, feeling out for something to steady her, to regain her footing. But there is only the grass . . .

Harper waits a second for Ida to finish. "Listen, Ida, how do we know this wasn't something you imagined afterward? Dreams can be very convincing."

"I thought of that," Ida says. "Maybe, I suppose. But what if I were to tell you my mother's killer was wearing a white mask of some kind? Sorta reminded me of a pillowcase, cut to size. Does that have any bearing on your case?"

Harper forces herself to remain nonchalant. She holds back from saying anything other than "Go on."

"Two holes for eyes," Ida says. "And I think a belt around his neck, holding it in place."

Harper clears her throat. "How do you know this?"

"Saw it, like I told you. It's really vivid, like I'm actually there. I see him as she saw him, hood and all. Walking toward her, looking like something out of a horror movie. But when she calls his name I can't hear it. It's muffled, as if I'm not meant to know."

Harper nods, listening, not quite able to believe her ears.

Eyes narrowed, Ida is doing her best to try to remember. "Either she couldn't find her voice, or I'm not listening hard enough. But it's not there. She calls him, turns around, sees him coming for her . . ." Ida's voice cracks and she casts her eyes away in shame. "Sorry."

"It's okay," Harper says.

When Ida looks up, there are tears streaming down her face. "I didn't talk about what I saw until years after my mother passed. I felt silly, as if I were lying to myself. But I knew deep down, it really did happen. I connected with her in some way, and experienced what had happened to her. I never really came to terms with my gift until after I'd spent time in the hospital, sorting my head out. Getting straight with myself."

"Have you had other experiences?"

"Yes. My grandpappy. When he died . . . I found him hanging, you know. After the ambulance took him away, I got up on a chair and took the rope down. When my hands touched it, I saw him looping it around his neck, weeping. He'd never gotten over my mother's death. It ate away at him until he couldn't take it any longer. I watched him prepare the noose, get everything ready. He kicked a stool out from under him and the rope bit in, as if it were a set of jaws. I'll never forget his eyes looking straight at me when I found him. Looking into me, as he knew *I* would be looking into *him*."

"It's not that I doubt what you're saying—" Harper starts to say.

"Stop." Ida looks Harper straight in the eyes. "Give me your hands."

"What—"

Ida's face says it all. Her cheeks clear of tears now. Eyes bright, and burning with an inner fire. Harper places her hands in Ida's, feeling completely out of her element. Out of control. She has surrendered herself to a woman she's only just met, and it goes against every fiber of her being, every instinct instilled in her through her training.

Ida's eyes roll back into her head as they close. She squeezes Harper's fingers. Harper is acutely aware of the air in the house, the jingle of a wind chime out on the porch, Ida's chest rising and falling steadily as she inhales, exhales, inhales, exhales. Again, the air in the house seems to grow warmer, thicker, and the light dimmer.

"Your partner has matching scars on his chest and back, where a bullet went straight through, narrowly missing his left lung and a crisscross of vital arteries. He calls it his miracle bullet and wears it on a silver chain. You asked him about it the first time you slept together."

Harper pulls her hands away, simultaneously repulsed by the way Ida has read her and disgusted with herself for acting as if Ida has done something wrong. She gets up, ready to run out of there, make her escape. But she can't—she's moved by what Ida revealed to her. The better part of her tells her she has to stay. She is confused.

"Sorry to scare you, sugar," Ida whispers. "But that's how it is."

Harper runs a hand over her face, feeling lost. "Can I use your bathroom?"

"Sure. Upstairs, first door on the right."

Harper runs up the stairs, goes in, and locks the door behind her. There's a mirrored sun catcher hanging in front of the window, splintering the daylight and sending it shimmering around the room. She takes a good, long look at herself in the mirror over the sink. Ida couldn't have known about Stu. How they'd talked about the bullet hanging around his neck.

"The miracle bullet," Harper whispers, thinking: *There has to be a reason she came chasing after me, got me back here. She said everyone's got ghosts. These girls are hers and they'll never be put to rest while the killer's still out there, doing what he wants. She'll always wake up in the middle of the night, picturing his hooded face coming toward her, seen through her mother's eyes . . .*

Harper heads back downstairs.

Ida turns around to look at her, face expectant. "Well?"

"Okay," Harper sighs.

◆ ◆ ◆

Ida closes Harper's car door, then leans on the frame. "Whatever I can do to help, I want to do it. I've spent a lot of years out here on my own, going to bed early. Jumping at shadows. Hoping a foul wind don't blow. I think I've kept out of the way for long enough."

Harper nods, just the once. "That old phone I saw in there work?"

"Yeah."

"Well, I'll call to let you know what's happening." She starts the engine, starts to leave, then stops. "Can I ask you something, Ida?"

"Sure."

"You ever wondered about him coming after you the way he did your mom?"

Ida's face grows heavy as stone. "All my life, sugar. All my life."

5

Gertie Wilson sits midway on the bus, earbuds in, Taylor Swift drowning out the noise from the engine and the other passengers.

A notification sounds in her ears. She looks at the cell phone.

It's a text from Hugo:

```
Why do we live on opposite sides of town?
☹
```

Gertie taps her reply and sends it in seconds.

```
Because it makes you miss me even more?
```

Hugo's reply is instant.

```
I always miss you. I don't stop thinking
about you. Does that make me sound like
a fucking stalker? LOL
```

Gertie smiles.

```
If you are then you're MY stalker. Can't
wait to see you tomorrow.
```

She looks out the window at the town rolling by. Gertie is the first in her family to attend college and do something other than work the dirt for a living. She plans to keep her hands clean.

Her phone pings.

```
Love you. Call me tonight XXX
```

Gertie's stop comes up, and she joins the half dozen people about to get off. The bus slows, the doors open, and they spill out. She would be glad to be free from the hot confines of the bus if it weren't raining. Gertie darts beneath the shelter of the bus stop and taps a reply.

```
Promise. Love you too, Hugo ☺ xxx
```

She riffles in her bag for her umbrella. It's a pocket-sized contraption that just about manages to keep the rain off her head and shoulders. The rest of her is getting steadily soaked. As she crosses the street and heads for home, walking by the side of the road, she can feel the water getting in her shoes, seeping in around her toes.

Her father continues to nag her about taking driving lessons and getting her license, and she's seriously considering it. Days like this, she could put her environmental concerns to one side if it means getting home dry. Her studies so far have incorporated the cause and effect of climate change. In all good conscience, she can't warrant expending the additional carbon just for her own comfort . . . but there comes a point, sometimes.

A car would make sense.

"Hey!"

The voice makes her jump. She looks to her right. A truck has slowed next to her, the window down so that the driver can call out to her.

She ignores him and continues walking.

"I *faid* hey!"

Gertie stops. "Can I help you?"

The rain drums down around her, beating the top of the umbrella.

"Are you going far? I could give you a lift. You look *foaked!*"

Gertie looks at the man. He appears harmless enough. Funny scar running along his top lip, lifting it up a shade to reveal his gums and teeth. "I'm okay, thanks."

"If you ain't got far to go, jump in," the man says. When she hesitates, he shrugs. "Look, I'm *juft* doin' my good *Famaritan* bit."

She knows she shouldn't. She knows it goes against every impulse to get in the man's car. But he looks honest enough. Perhaps even a little simple. "I just live up the road," she tells him, getting closer to the driver's-side window.

"That farm up there? I know it."

Now she remembers his truck driving past her the day before. He really does drive through there on a regular basis. Perhaps he even knows her parents . . .

"Yeah it's not far," she says, deciding. "Are you sure you don't mind? I'm pretty soaked. I don't want to ruin the inside of your car."

The man laughs. "*Thif* old thing?"

Gertie walks around to the passenger side and gets in. The man waits for her to buckle herself up, then takes off. The wipers just push sheets of water around the windshield; the rain is falling so heavy.

"Thanks for doing this," Gertie tells him. "It's not often someone does something for someone else around here."

"I know what you mean," the man says. "There are *fome* rude people out there."

"Do you live far?"

"Out∫ide of town. Got my own place."

"Married? Kids?"

The man guffaws like a simpleton next to her. "Go∫h no!"

Gertie laughs along with him, the ice broken between them. "Ah, this is my place coming up on the left. My daddy owns most of this."

"One of them big-time farmer∫, huh?"

"You could say that," Gertie says, frowning as the man drives straight past her front gate. "Hey, uh, that was it back there."

"Oh ∫hit! Here, let me turn thi∫ old girl around," he tells her, slowing the car and bumping it up on the mud. He turns the steering wheel, as if he's getting ready to do a U-turn and head back the way they've come. Gertie looks back through the rain-smeared window at her front gate.

So close to it.

"I can get out and run along, it's no—"

Gertie feels a sudden sharp pain in the side of her neck. She turns to look at the man. He holds a syringe in his hand, face studying her.

She tries to open the car door, manages it, but only halfway. Gertie swings one leg out, and that's as far as she gets. Going any farther is impossible, as if her limbs are filled with lead. She struggles to keep her eyes open and can hear her own heartbeat in her ears as she watches the man get out, run around the front of the truck, and tuck her right leg back inside. He closes the door, then runs back to his own side. Now they're moving.

She can't keep her eyes open any longer. It's creeping up on her, like a warm hand on the back of her head. She looks at the man. It *is* a hand. He is stroking her hair.

"∫leep."

The Gator's Snap has a distinctive *eau de broken toilet*—a combo of sweaty work shirts, tired feet in old shoes, bad aftershave, smoke, more smoke, and spilled beer. But despite the questionable hygiene of such a darkened, musty establishment, it *is* a cop hangout. Only lawmakers and retired lawmakers frequent The Gator's Snap, which means it's free of drug dealers in the toilets, old hookers working the tables looking to score for the night, and dubious under-the-counter transactions. Midweek it can get quiet in there, so Harper isn't surprised to find it fairly empty when Harper walks in, shaking off her umbrella. She spots Stu right away, his back to her at the bar, nursing his drink. She plops herself down next to him.

The bartender, Lenny, works every night, without fail. He wears a T-shirt cut off at the arms, showing off his large biceps. The one on the left carries an inscription: "Ma." The one on the right bears the likeness of The Boss, accompanied by stars and stripes.

"Still rainin' out there?" Stu asks her.

"Cats and dogs."

"Hey Jane," Lenny says. "What're you having?"

She runs her fingers through her hair—it's been a trying day, and she feels unhinged. "Something strong, Len."

"Like that, huh?" he asks, fixing her drink.

"Could say that," Harper says. Stu glances sideways at her. He's finishing up his usual, pouring the last of the whiskey down his throat. "And another of whatever he's drinking."

"Got it."

Stu watches Lenny refill his glass. As usual, he's overgenerous with the measure—no doubt one of the main reasons cops keep coming back. Lenny sets their drinks down.

"Thanks," Harper says as Lenny moves off, busying himself wiping down the tables, collecting errant glasses.

When he's sure that the bartender is out of earshot, Stu produces a notebook and turns to the last written page. He speaks in a low voice. "I've been busy. I've made a list of everyone who fabricated a report."

"Oh?"

"Yeah. One of the names on there you will recognize right away," Stu says. "Hal Crenna."

Harper's eyebrows rise to peaks. "The mayor?"

"Well, mayor hopeful. He's runnin' for it, and from what I've heard through the grapevine, there's a strong chance he'll make it, too," Stu says. "What we got would sink him before he's even afloat."

He pushes the notebook toward her.

"All these names," Harper says. The cover-up includes not only the actual investigating officers, but the captains and chiefs at the time. "When we reveal this, the PD is going to come under some intense scrutiny, I can tell you."

"About time, maybe?"

Harper sighs. "The reasoning behind it, that it was to protect the town . . . it just doesn't wash. Sure, a murder here would impact tourism. Maybe for a little while. But eventually Hope's Peak would recover. Things pass. I have to believe there was something more to it."

"When we've caught this guy, I think we should pay Hal Crenna a visit."

"Amen to that."

Stu says, "So I take it you went to see Ida Lane . . ."

"I did," Harper says.

"How'd it go?"

She can't shake her last words to Ida: *You ever wondered about him coming after you?*

And Ida's reply: *All my life.*

"She's a woman who's spent her whole life in fear. Lived away from town, kept to herself, has a television and a phone, and little else. Ida's off the grid, Stu. About as off the grid as you can get, bar moving out to the woods and living in a shack."

"Jesus."

Harper takes a hearty swallow of her drink. For her nerves, to settle them after her experience at Ida's. She's aware of the tremor in her right hand and hopes Stu hasn't noticed. It'll pass. Might take another couple of drinks . . . but it'll pass.

She hopes.

"There's something else, Stu, and I need you to be open-minded about it."

He frowns. "Go on."

"Remember what Claymore said? About her touching her mother's hand and passing out?"

"Yeah."

"Well it wasn't just shock. She claims she had some kind of . . . vision, I guess you could call it. She told me how she witnessed her mother's murder. The killer coming for her, forcing her down on the ground. The whole thing. She's relived it all these years, in her dreams. Over, and over, and over."

Stu smiles. "Jane, you don't believe this, do you? I'm sure it's just some kind of trauma. I mean, that's quite a thing to go through as a kid."

"There's more."

He looks at her. "What's gotten into you? You're not usually like this . . ."

Harper leans in close, her eyes locked with his, voice lowered. "She told me the killer wore a white sack on his head, holes cut out for eyes. Belt around his neck."

He knocks back what he has in his glass, almost gasping from the hit but needing it. "Who else have you told?" he whispers.

"No one but you. There's no way she came up with that on her own. But that's not the weirdest part."

"I don't know if I want to hear this."

"You need to," Harper says. "Stu, you need to hear this."

"Alright."

She takes a deep breath. "She detailed the bullet wound you got. The way you wear the bullet around your neck. And how we talked about it the first night we slept together."

Stu gets up, walks to the door without another word. Harper goes after him. The night air has a chill to it. Chasing a stiff drink, it's refreshing for Stu to feel it on his face, filling his lungs. He fumbles for a cigarette from his jacket pocket.

"I thought you quit?" Harper asks him.

"I did."

He lights up. Harper can see he's about as unnerved as she was. "You okay?"

Stu blows smoke out into the night. It meets the black and comes apart. "I don't know. You?"

"I'm getting there. Freaked me out, I have to say. It was just so unexpected. And uncanny. How can she know this stuff if she doesn't have some kind of gift?"

Stu doesn't say anything. He smokes and chews it over.

"It happens when she touches things. Her mother's body. My hands," Harper says. "Her grandfather hung himself. When she touched the rope, she saw him committing suicide. It's connected to physical contact."

"Okay."

"You alright with this so far?"

He shakes his head, blowing smoke. "Yes. No. I don't know, Jane."

"Well, you haven't heard the nutty part yet."

Stu's eyebrows rise. "I *haven't*!?"

"I want to take Ida to the morgue, to see what she can get from Alma Buford."

Now Stu shakes his head for real. He drops his cigarette, stubs it out on the concrete. "Absolutely not, Jane. I can't let you do it."

She holds his arm in a firm grip and forces him to look at her. "I want you to help me get in. You know one of the guys there, right?"

"Damn, Jane . . . you realize that not only is it completely immoral, we could lose our jobs because of it?"

"Yeah, but we won't. Anyway, she's only going to put her hands on Alma's body. Just to see what she picks up on," Harper says. "Please, Stu. Help me do this. I'm convinced Ida has something, something we can't explain, something that is some kind of gift. I think she's meant to help solve these murders."

He looks away. Harper grabs his chin, turns his face back to hers, and plants a long, hard kiss on his lips.

"What was that for?"

"For being you, and trying to steer me right."

"And have I?" Stu asks her.

She smiles. Gives him one more quick peck. "Nope. But you keep trying and that's what matters, stud."

"Listen, Jane, I don't know when they're moving the body. Or when I can get us in there, if I can at all. But I'll try my best," Stu tells her.

Harper opens the door to the Snap. "Come on stud, let's go back inside. I'll buy you a nightcap."

"I think I need it."

She stops. "Stu, you should meet her. Make up your own mind. I'm skeptical, but . . . there's that part of me that believes what she's saying. That believes her as a person."

Stu leads the way to the bar. "Yeah, okay, let's have a drink first, though, eh?"

The sun has not yet risen. A faded band of light has crept in on the horizon, revealing the hazy green smudges that delineate stretches of woods. Above that, the sky is still dark blue and, directly overhead, it is darker yet. The stars are burning bright, making the most of their moment to shine before the dawn forces them back.

Gerry Fischer gets out of his truck, flashlight in hand. A half hour before, he got a call from a friend passing through. He mentioned seeing a truck parked at the side of the road, thought it was suspicious—he drove past it so fast he never got a good look at the make, model, or plate. Gerry has worked his land for close to twenty years; it's not the first time he's gone out in the early morning to see about trespassers. He stands at the edges of the field, endless rows of soybeans, waist-high and lush green. Gerry reaches out with his flashlight. The light lands on something at the edge of its beam.

He walks through the soybeans, making straight for it. Most likely some kids were out here, fucking around. It's probably a beer can or a packet of condoms.

How can kids these days go through a packet of condoms? What's the world coming to, Gerry wonders, approaching the object where it lies on the soft soil. Only it's not a single object. It's a shoe . . . It's attached to a leg.

Harper wakes, looks at the time on her phone: 3:15 a.m.

She groans, sitting up, rubbing at her head. She can't sleep for any real length of time. Her head hums from the drink, from the conflict of her own heart saying good-bye to Stu last night outside her apartment building. The way he swooped in for a kiss and she pulled back, telling him her head was all over the place, it didn't feel right, she didn't know what she wanted. The little pecks she gave him at the bar were not meant to be taken as anything but a friendly gesture. Stu thought they were building up to something more impressive—and he can't understand why she's blowing cold with him.

What do I want?

Harper goes to the kitchen and fetches a glass of water from the tap. She chases it with a few aspirins, and washes those down with more water. Harper stands by the sideboard, wanting to sleep, knowing she can't.

It feels as though she's led Stu on, giving him hope that what they've been doing would lead to something deeper. Sleeping with him, getting close, but never once telling him that she loves him. She has feelings for him, misses him in her bed, misses his touch . . . but at the same time, there's something pulling her away, keeping him at arm's length. Harper craves his affection, the comfort of being intimate with him. And yet she knows that's different from wanting to be in a relationship.

There are times she wishes she'd stayed in San Francisco. Her whole reason for leaving in the first place had been to flee her broken marriage.

What will I do if Stu and I don't work out? Run to another town? Another city? Pull up stakes and take off every time a relationship goes south?

The clock on the kitchen wall ticks away, keeping the tempo of the time slipping from her grip, running like sand through her fingers.

Her cell phone rings, making her jump out of her skin. Harper swipes the screen and answers, pressing the cell to her ear.

Thirty minutes later, she and Stu are on the road.

The rain has stopped and the dawn is setting the horizon ablaze, but neither detective is in a mood to appreciate it. Stu rubs his forehead.

"Hey, why don't you take the aspirin in the glove compartment?" Harper asks him.

"I don't like takin' pills," Stu says obstinately.

Harper rolls her eyes. "Christ, Stu. They're not pills. Not like *that*, anyway. They'll help with the headache."

He straightens. "What headache?"

Give me strength . . .

"You're an ass, you know that?"

Stu looks out the passenger window. "Yep."

They arrive at Gerry Fischer's land, and Harper pulls in behind a patrol car with the lights running. A forensics team is already on the scene, their van in front of the black-and-white. They've set up lights on stands in the field to the left.

Stu and Harper climb out. The passenger-side door of the patrol car is open. One of the police officers is sitting with his legs planted on the ground, head down, looking sorry for himself. His partner waves them down and approaches with his hands on his belt, as if he's an old-time lawman in a long-gone frontier town. "Mornin'."

"This is Stu Raley. I'm Jane Harper." They both show their ID badges. Harper nods in the direction of the man perched on the passenger seat. "What's up with him?"

"He don't handle the stiffs too well."

Stu shares a look with her. "Uh-huh."

The officer shakes hands with them. "I'm Weinberg. That there is Tasker."

"Tasker, huh?" Stu asks, looking away as he mumbles something inaudible under his breath.

Weinberg leans in close. "On the job eight months. Know what I'm sayin'?"

"I see," Harper says. "Tell me about the body."

"Gerry Fischer works this land. All this is soybean," Weinberg explains, indicating the rows of vegetation around them. "He got a call in the night. Something about a car parked out here."

"Right," Harper says, looking back to where CSU has set up the lights. "Then what?"

"Got here, found the body. Female, probably late teens, early twenties," Weinberg says.

Stu scratches his forehead. "Coroner here yet?"

"ME's on his way."

Harper pats Officer Weinberg on the arm. "Alright, we're gonna go have a look. You boys had better stick around."

"Sure, Detective. We've got orders to remain here until the crime scene is secured."

"Good."

As they pass Tasker, the young officer looks decidedly green around the gills. Harper leads Stu Raley into the field where CSU is working. Under the intense illumination they have erected around the body, the girl looks like the centerpiece of a dramatic theater production. The soybean stalks cast spidery shadows over the girl, and, as with Alma Buford, she looks as if she is sleeping. But the bruises on her neck say otherwise; the purple handprints are so clear, Harper can make out the actual shape of fingers in the dead girl's flesh. The crown sits lopsided on her head, as if it slipped after the killer set it there.

Stu looks visibly disturbed by the blood that has run from the girl's privates and onto her clothes. The killer managed to close her eyes, but there was nothing he could do about her mouth—it remains agape, open in an expression of frozen terror. "Fuck."

Harper squats down next to the girl, careful not to get near the mud. She looks at her, then up at Stu.

"We have to stop this."

6

By the time Stu Raley catches a ride with CSU back to Hope's Peak PD, the sun has risen and Harper wishes she could have San Francisco's climate back—cool in the day, even cooler at night. In some way, Harper misses the fog rolling in off the bay. She misses eating out in Chinatown. But there are bad memories, too. Things she'd rather forget.

The car bounces along the dirt road leading to Gerry Fischer's farmhouse. It's an impressive spread of buildings against a never-ending backdrop of crops. Far as the eye can see, rows and rows of short green soybeans.

A text comes through on her cell.

Just heading to the station now—SR

Harper smiles, despite the situation. *Another dead girl. There's no stopping the killer now. Whatever it was that held him at bay in recent years is gone. He has the taste, the thirst, and needs to quench it.*

Serial killers are like any other addict—they have to kill again. It's a need.

Harper gets out and walks toward the farmhouse. Gerry Fischer opens the door and shakes her hand.

"Mister Fischer? I'm Detective Jane Harper with Hope's Peak PD."

"Mornin', Detective. You can call me Gerry," he tells her.

"Okay."

"You want coffee or somethin'?"

As it is, Harper still feels the hum of a hangover. She didn't get enough sleep, she drank too much the night before, the dead girl is very much on her mind, and the heat is weighing down on her. It sticks to you, makes you feel dirty and sweaty in no time at all.

"I'd like that," she tells him. Gerry shows her inside. To Harper's relief, he has his air-conditioning on and the house is cool. He leads her into the dining room and instructs her to take a seat at the big table in there.

"Cream and sugar?"

Harper nods her head. "Yes, please."

"Won't be a minute. Then I guess you'll have some questions for me, won't ya?"

"I'm afraid so, yes."

Gerry leaves her alone while he goes to the kitchen. Harper scans the room. There are pictures of Gerry and his wife—some include their kids, some solo shots of the children as they got older. She guesses that they've all left home and moved away by now. Gerry Fischer has to be in his late fifties.

He returns carrying two mugs of freshly brewed coffee and sets them down. "There ya are. Hope that's to yer likin'."

"Thanks."

He sits. "So . . ."

Harper places her recorder on the table between them, opens her notepad, and removes the cap from her pen. "I'll try to keep this as brief as possible, Mister Fischer. There might be further questions later on, as you can imagine."

"Sure."

"Let's start at the beginning. Tell me what happened last night."

Gerry slurps his coffee, then explains the course of events; to Harper, it is pretty straightforward. He discovered the young woman out there in the field and called it right in.

"And how long have you worked this land?" she asks him, taking notes.

"Twenty years. I have a dozen or so men helpin' me out. My wife handles the financials, ya know. I've always been more the, uh, *outdoors* type I guess you'd say," Gerry explains. His voice warbles in his throat and as he looks away, Harper is sure she can see tears in his eyes. "Ain't never had nothin' like this happen before, I can tell ya. Fucking awful thing to happen to such a young girl."

"Can you provide me with a list of your crew?" Harper asks him.

Gerry shrugs. "Can do. I've got nothin' to hide, and I know they ain't either. They're all good, reliable men. And anyway, if they were gonna rape and kill some young woman . . . they wouldn't leave her where they work, would they?"

"I seriously doubt it," Harper says. "But regardless of that, I do need to know all the facts. It's just part of the job."

"Yeah, I get that."

"Good," Harper says. She pushes the notepad to one side for the moment and lifts her coffee cup. "This won't harm your business in any way, will it?"

"I don't know. It's without precedent, ain't it?" Gerry says. "In either case, I'm more concerned with that girl. Who was she? How did she get there?"

Harper sighs. "That's what we're going to determine, believe me."

After an hour, Harper has asked all the questions she can think of. Gerry Fischer shows her out, and by now the sun is riding high. Away to the left, one of the fields is bare, save for the most crows Harper has ever seen in her life. There must be fifty of them, all picking over the dirt, some flapping their wings intermittently, a few cawing.

"I've never seen so many in one place," Harper tells Gerry, slipping her shades on. The sight of so many crows has sent a shiver up her spine. It's as if they have flocked to the Fischer land because there's been a death.

"Yeah, they get like that. That field will be planted next season. Crows peck at all the old seed."

Harper gestures toward the other fields, all lush green with life. "Obviously, we had heavy rainfall last night, but how do you get water to all these? Especially when it's hot like it is now. You've gotta have a steady supply, am I right?"

"Yeah and no," Gerry says, walking her to her car. "Ya see, what most people don't know is how to look at it. It ain't about how much water you can get to the field . . . it's about how much excess you can get rid of. Drainage is the biggest challenge we face out here sometimes."

"Right," Harper says, knowing what he means. Where does the water have to go when the land is so flat and featureless? "Well, thank you for your time, Gerry. As I said, any more questions, someone will be in touch."

"Got it."

"Please refrain from talking to the press for the time being. Though we can't tell you not to, we'd really appreciate it if you didn't just yet."

Gerry shoos her off. "Get away, girl. Any of them reporter types turn up here, I just might introduce 'em to Mary Sue."

Harper opens the car door, frowning. "Who's Mary Sue?"

"My shotgun," Gerry says with a grin.

One hand on the wheel, Harper swipes her phone and dials Stu's number.

"Hey," he says.

"I've finished up with the farmer. It was a bit of a dead end. I don't believe he knows any more than what he's told me already. I'll meet up with Albie at the ME's office. Mike's doing the girl's autopsy."

"You want me to come along?"

"I think I've got it covered."

"I might as well carry on with these files, then," Stu says. "CSU found a cell phone tucked into her pocket. It was waterlogged, but I'm hoping Albie might be able to do something with it. Otherwise we can pull her records from the network, but that'll take time."

"Okay." She drives with the fields on either side of her, crops towering nearly six feet in height, barely moving because of the lack of breeze. Deep green, the thick stems are rooted into the richest soil the United States has to offer. It feels as though she has parted the sea, headed for salvation on the other side.

If only that were the case.

"How's the file work going?" Harper asks Stu.

"I'm keeping a list of the major differences between the official and unofficial records. It'll help in prosecuting the men who covered this up for so long, but so far I haven't picked up on anything substantial. Nothing that's a case breaker."

"Okay. Well, keep digging at it."

"Listen. About last night at the bar—"

Harper shakes her head. "Not yet, Stu. We'll talk about it later, I promise. You have my word. But not right now. I can't deal with that as well as watching a young girl get cut open."

His voice is quieter. Distant. "Sure. I understand. We'll take a rain check. Talk to you later, kiddo."

The line goes dead before Harper can say anything else.

When Harper walks into the medical examiner's with Albie, Mike has already set about meticulously going over the victim's body. Captain Morelli has decided to attend. He glowers in the corner, leaning against the wall with his hands in his pockets.

"I don't usually attend these, but for this one, I want to see his handiwork for myself," Morelli says.

Not much to see, Harper thinks. *Apart from jizz and hair strands, the killer's a relatively tidy trooper.*

Mike works alongside Kara to determine for certain the young woman's cause of death, though it's brutally clear. Strangled. The purple blossoms on her neck are proof of that. Mike examines the girl's fingernails. He looks at Harper. "No skin this time. Just wet dirt. Her nails are clogged with it."

The awful tragedy of the girl on the slab, her body icy cold and dull, is something Harper can't get out of her head. When you see a cadaver, you still expect them to breathe. It doesn't make sense that their chest doesn't rise and fall as it should—that when you touch them there is no heat at all. Just the coolness of flesh that no longer convulses and has become heavy as marble. A room is just a room until there is the unthinkable presence of a dead body within it. Then it assumes the quiet stillness of an empty church, as if the very air around the body regards its existence there—what it was, what it is, and what it will become.

Samples of the soil will go to CSU to see if it matches the soil at the crime scene. Harper knows it will. It doesn't fit the killer's MO to move a body postmortem. He does what he needs to do, kills them, and leaves them. That's it. The killer does not concern himself with moving a body from one location to another—for what point?

"Any ID on the body?" Morelli asks.

Mike shakes his head. "Dental records drew a blank, as did DNA. At the moment, she's plain old Jane Doe."

"Great," Morelli says. "Let's just hope there's a missing person's on file or we're gonna end up canvassing the area. That could take time we don't have."

Mike starts cutting, the scalpel slipping through the girl's brown skin as though it were delicate as jelly. Dark blood pools in the scalpel's wake. Albie turns around, face suddenly green with nausea. "I'm step-ping out."

"Okay," Harper says, privately amused.

The captain waits for Albie to clear the room before letting loose a big growly sigh. "How can you let yourself get sickened by a little blood and guts? Pussy."

"I think it's that the victim's a young girl, sir," Harper suggests.

"Can't argue with you there," the captain says. "Damn, this is going to cause a major shit storm."

Harper stands next to him and lowers her voice. "The killer's gain-ing momentum, for whatever reason. What used to be a dead girl turn-ing up every three or four years has turned into three in only a handful of months," Harper says. "This is the third victim on my watch."

"The press is after our asses. And they'll get them, too, if we can't deliver a culprit," Morelli says.

Harper watches Mike peel back the girl's skin to explore her innards. A familiar gaminess rises from the opened cadaver; the smell of dead, lifeless meat exposed to the air is not something you get used to. But it is something you can grow to stomach, ignoring it so you don't vomit.

She looks at the captain—he's aged in a matter of days. His eyelids hang loose, face drawn in, body sagging with exhaustion. Some of it, she knows, due in no small part to the stress of those files. Of putting his trust in her hands and hoping she does the right thing with what she finds. "Have you slept, sir?"

He smiles. It's weak and there's nothing in it, a truly empty gesture. "Not much."

Mike examines the girl's cold heart and Harper thinks: *I won't tonight.*

"Can I have a word in private?" she asks, opening the door to the corridor outside. Morelli follows her out. "Sorry, I didn't want Mike and Kara to hear."

"Spit it out, Detective."

"It's the files, sir. There's no way of protecting the men who have covered this up all these years. Stu and myself will be presenting our findings and recommending prosecution," Harper tells him. "This could reflect badly on you, too. I thought you should know that."

Morelli runs a hand over his face. "When bodies started showing up again, I brought you into the fold, did I not?"

"Yes sir. But if you'd presented your evidence earlier, the deaths of those two young women might've been avoided."

Morelli rubs at the tired corners of his eyes. "What do you want me to say, Detective? You think I don't know all that?"

"Sir . . ."

Morelli shakes his head. "Another time. Right now, we have a killer to apprehend. After, when the dust has settled, we can start pointing fingers at the men who have protected this town for three decades, okay? It's easy playing the righteous card when your hands are nice and clean. Well, mine were dirty before I had a chance to start, so spare me your condemnation," he says, storming off.

The captain's car peels out of the parking lot. Albie and Harper let him go on ahead, not wanting to tail him the whole way. Albie starts the engine. "Doesn't always get me like that," he says defensively.

"Everyone gets a bit queasy now and then," Harper says. She hasn't felt ill at the sight of a dead body since her first corpse back when she was a newbie. Even then, she got through the experience without spewing her guts up. Albie still looks green around the gills. "You realize you've gotta find a way of soldiering through it, though, right?"

"I know. I find fresh air helps," he says.

"Of course," she says, still replaying her conversation with Morelli.

Albie backs the car out. "It's not the smell or anything. It's just . . . I find it hard to watch."

"I hear you," Harper says. "I've got to admit it's never bothered me. I know the smell is there, and it's god-awful, but I just block it out."

It's not just the smell . . . it's the dehumanizing of the process. Watching another human being rendered down and filleted, little more than meat. Watching an autopsy makes you confront all the sick reality beneath the surface. An elderly woman, her wrinkled skin peeled back, the coroner's scalpel slicing down to the bone. A young boy, so full of life and potential, stripped down to parts.

"Lucky."

Yeah, till later, when I can't stop thinking about them.

They head back to the station, the last of the daylight sitting out on the edges of the world, hanging in a reddish haze behind the trees. On the East Coast, the dusk is royal blue, like mist rolling out on a lake at night.

"When we get back, I've got something for you. CSU found a phone on her. It's got water damage. I want you to try and get in there, see what you can pull from it."

He cocks an eyebrow. "Not sure if I'll be able to get anything."

"Just give it a shot, okay? Don't make me have to go to the asshole phone company and request their data," Harper says.

"I can try, boss," Albie says. He checks the mirror, changes lanes. Flexes his hands on the wheel. "You drove down to Chalmer, didn't you?" he asks.

Harper shifts in the passenger seat. "Dead end," she says, dismissing it. "Waste of the gas driving there."

Albie shakes his head. "Ain't that the way, huh?"

"I don't suppose you've had luck tracking sales of DXM."

"Not when every Tom, Dick, and Harry can go online and order it. It's not like ketamine, which we can trace, to an extent. This crap is everywhere."

"And readily available . . . any luck following up on Alma's friends?" Harper asks.

"Nope. They were all pretty normal. No boyfriends that anyone knows of."

Harper sighs. "Damn."

"Hopefully we turn up a name for girl number three," Albie says.

Harper thinks: *girl eleven.*

"Yeah. It'd be real nice to catch whoever's behind this and put this case to bed," Harper says. "Trouble is, I don't think we'll be that lucky."

Harper walks into Captain Morelli's office to find John Dudley sitting there.

"Oh," she says. "It's you."

The corner of Dudley's mouth lifts in what could be classified as a smile. "Last time I checked."

She takes a seat. "Morelli running late? We were just following him from the ME's office."

Dudley shrugs. "Not my turn to babysit."

They wait, the silence between them stretching out. Harper can't stand it any longer and says something—anything—just to break it. "Hey, John? I know we don't always see eye to eye. But you've been a big help on this case. Getting hold of those white supremacists."

"Thanks. I suppose we clash sometimes. It happens. I don't take it personally."

It's one of several occasions on which Dudley has surprised her. She always considered him a dick. Now she's not so sure.

Maybe I was just a bitch for thinking it without giving the guy a chance.

"That's good to hear," she says.

Harper looks at the clock on the wall, ticking away, and when she turns back to him, he has a smile on his face. It should look cute, perhaps. But there's something about it that doesn't fit with the rest of him, as if smiling doesn't come naturally to a man like John Dudley.

Shortly after she transferred to Hope's Peak, Dudley made a play for Harper. They were in a car, heading to rendezvous with Stu at a crime scene. He asked her what she did outside of work. When Harper said she didn't get out too much, he asked her if she wanted to go for a drink sometime, and before she could answer, he had his hand on her knee. Harper froze for a moment as she wrestled with what to do next. She gently lifted his hand from her leg and, in the politest terms, told Dudley she was not interested. Thank you anyway.

He didn't take it very well—and the atmosphere between them has been frosty ever since, particularly since he caught wind that she and Stu were "seeing" each other . . .

Morelli and Stu walk in. The captain goes straight to his desk, oblivious to any atmosphere lurking between the two detectives. Stu senses it right away. He looks at Dudley, then Harper.

She gives him a look: *Don't say anything. Sit your ass down.*

Thankfully, as Morelli starts to question them regarding aspects of the case, Stu does just that. He sits between Harper and Dudley.

Once the general details of their investigation are out of the way, Morelli looks at Dudley.

"If you'd give us a minute, Detective."

"Huh?"

Morelli indicates the door to his office, his hand held out, palm up. "If you would, John."

"Oh." Dudley stands, looks at Harper and Raley, then leaves. The door clicks shut behind him.

Captain Morelli pops a candy in his mouth and rolls it around. "I've gotta do a press conference on live TV. I'm trying to hold those bloodsuckers off, but you two know how these things are. They're par for the course."

"Yes sir," Stu says.

"So, at some point, I'm going to be telling the country we have a killer here in Hope's Peak," Morelli says. "How are you doing with those files? Are they much use?"

"Yes and no," Harper tells him. "Raley has made a list of everyone who helped cover this up."

"Yeah?"

Harper thinks back to her conversation with the captain at the ME's office. "As I said earlier today, there's going to be a lot of fallout from this. More than for the murders themselves, I expect."

"One of the big names is that of Hal Crenna. He's a former captain of police who worked his way up from the bottom. Now he's about to become mayor of Hope's Peak," Stu says. "At least, it's looking that way."

Morelli nods. "I know Hal."

"Back in the day, Crenna falsified two of the reports in those files you gave us. That revelation would put his career aspirations on permanent hold," Stu says.

"You don't have to tell me that, Detective," Morelli snaps. "But like I said earlier to your partner here, the main focus has to be stopping these murders. Then, and only then, can we deal with the corruption in the department. If that means I have to step away from this position, then so be it."

Harper leans forward, hands clasped between her knees. "Sir, neither of us believes you're dirty. But there's been a big cover-up here, and I'm not sure why. There's protecting the town, but this goes beyond that. I think someone knew the identity of the killer, and that's why the deaths of these girls had to be swept under the rug."

"Well, I know one thing," Morelli says, crunching through the candy. "Right now, in the eyes of the public, we're chasing our tails here. We are unable to protect the citizens of this town from a sexual predator and murderer."

"All the more reason to do a press conference, sir," Harper tells him. "Get the word out there. If we get some exposure, it might stay the killer's hand long enough for us to catch him."

Morelli looks at her. "The operable word here being 'might.'"

Leaving the captain's office, Harper feels a hand on her arm.

Stu steers her to the left, to one of the supply closets. He yanks the pull cord, the single bulb illuminating the dingy confines of the tiny room, and shuts the door.

"What's up?" she asks him.

He's flustered. Red in the face. "All that about the TV interviews? I hope it's made you rethink what you're planning on doing."

"What d'you mean? Taking Ida to see the body?"

He rolls his eyes. "What else? Come on, Jane. See sense here. If the press gets wind that you've marched a goddamn psychic into the morgue, public confidence will plummet. They'll eat us alive. And that's not the worst. If they put two and two together and realize she's the daughter of a victim—"

"Look, even *if* that happens, they won't make the connection. As far as they're aware, Ruby Lane isn't connected to the case. At least, not until we expose the truth at some point. Going on the assumption we ever catch the guy . . ."

"Ida is a soothsayer. Nothing more. Having her anywhere near the investigation makes it look like we're relying on voodoo or some other nonsense, rather than good old-fashioned police work," Stu tells her. He crosses his arms, looks down at the floor. When Harper reaches out and holds his shoulders, Stu looks back up at her. "What?"

"I hear you. Honestly, I do. But I can't do this without you. I want to break this case. So far, all we have are bits and pieces. I think we're on the verge of something here. I need you with me."

The silence stretches out, and for a moment, she wonders if he will turn her down, but he nods once, frowning.

"Okay," he says. "But I do this out of respect for you as my partner, not for anything else."

That hurts, but she takes it on the chin. "Okay. You're not letting your personal feelings get in the way. I respect that."

"Good."

"I just hope all this isn't about me blowing hot and cold with you, Stu. Because I have my reasons. I'm not your ex-wife, okay?" Harper says.

"I know, I know," he says.

Harper opens the door. "Come on, before someone wonders why we're standing in a closet."

7

The road is a dark river through the night and she rides the current.

Ida sits forward against the steering wheel, concentrating on the asphalt. Driving at night has never been her forte, and for once, she will be glad to be off the back roads. There's something comfortable about joining the flow of traffic at night, the beams of opposing headlights giving a false sense of security she nonetheless buys into. She has the radio on—the station is playing an old Leonard Cohen number she knows but can't put a name to. In that way, old songs are like old friends you meet in the street. You talk for a while, having genuine back-and-forth, all the while trying to remember what they're called.

The detective told her to get to the Buy N Save in Hope's Peak at eleven. She knows her watch runs five or six minutes fast, and even *that* is telling her she's late.

It's my fault.

Ida was set to go. She'd thrown some stuff in the truck, made sure everything was switched off in the house, closed all the windows, was about to leave when she was positively crippled with fear. She opened the screen door, and an invisible hand took her gut and wrenched it around, twisted it up tight. Ida doubled over in pain, stumbled back, the door swinging shut. There in the darkness of her house, she found she could not move. Could not go near the door.

Come on. One step at a time.

She tried, she really did. Yet the thought of getting out there, of heading into the night on her own, with the prospect of being in the presence of a dead body, scared her more than anything had in a long while. Even the dreams did not have the toxic effect the fear was having on her then.

More than anything, she knew what was coming. Ida had spent years revisiting her mother's murder, over and over. Now she would experience another murder. Another little sparrow that had had its neck wrung. Laid to rest in a field, coveted as a thing of beauty and venerated as such. But they were what they were. Nothing more than strangled birds, silenced before they knew their own song.

It was the thought of them as helpless birds that got her back on her feet, that made her draw a heavy breath and charge at the door, keys clenched in her hand so hard she nearly drew blood. Those young women deserved to have their stories heard. Their songs would remain unwritten otherwise. Ida was on the road without even realizing it, gunning the engine, knuckles white on the steering wheel. She'd sped her way through a mile or two before she relaxed her grip and fell to her own anxieties of the dark night around her.

But the fire inside her had already been lit. Whatever awaited her, whatever the latest victim had to tell her, she would listen.

Harper waits while Stu dozes on and off next to her in the car.

"Keeping you up?" she asks, giving him a sharp elbow in the ribs when his head lowers, chin resting on his chest, a stifled snore coming from his crumpled mouth.

"Huh?" Stu looks around, eyes red, and wipes his mouth on the back of his hand. "Did I nod off again?"

"Either that or you were slipping into a coma, Stu."

"Sorry."

Harper checks the time: 11:46. She wonders if Ida will show. She sounded game on the phone when she spoke to her earlier, but something could have changed since then.

"Feeling it at the moment. I don't know, I can't sleep at home," Stu says, stretching out. "Do you get that? When you're caught up in the case?"

She knows he means "the victims" when he talks about the case. A death is like a boat cutting through water, the ensuing pain and heartache left in its wake fanning out for a long time to come. But she knows there's something else, too.

Us.

"Stu, I said we'd have that chat. I think maybe—"

He cuts in. "D'you know me and Karen were high school sweethearts? Prom dates even? Man, I thought it was the happiest day of my life, getting married to her. Went off without a hitch. Everything was rosy. I worked my way up to detective over time. We got our first house. A place of our own. You know that feeling? When you go from renting someplace to actually owning a piece of one yourself?"

"I do."

His eyes are glassy, looking through the windshield, lost in the fog of what he's saying. "I thought we'd last, I really did. But you know what? Sometimes it just don't work out. I tried giving her a kid, Jane. I tried to make the picture complete, but I couldn't."

"How do you know the problem was with you?" Harper asks. "Maybe she couldn't—"

Stu shakes his head. "No. It was me."

"Is that what's eating you up? Some kind of fucking guilt?" Harper slaps him on the arm with the back of her hand. It brings him back. "Look at me. Stu, really look at me."

Stu's voice is only a whisper. His eyes hang heavy. "Yes?"

"You are not to blame for your marriage ending. No more than I'm to blame for mine. We make decisions—sometimes those decisions turn out to be mistakes. That's just how it is," Harper says.

"I know."

"Why have you brought all this up? Because of us?"

"God, Jane, do I have to spell it out? I've got feelings for you. I want us to be more than what we are. I thought that was going to happen, but all I get now is a cold shoulder. You don't want to know," Stu tells her. "I wonder what's wrong with me that I have this effect . . ."

"Fuck's sake." Harper grabs his hand, gives it a hard squeeze. At that moment a car's headlights sweep across the parking lot. It's Ida's truck. "This is her. Listen to me, Stu. It's not you. I think my own insecurities are the problem. I've got a history of running away when things don't turn out the way I wanted them to. I won't do that this time."

"Really?"

She smiles, though there's a sickening feeling in her gut from making such a promise—the problem is that you feel compelled to keep promises like that. "Really."

"What about Karen?"

She shrugs. "It'll sort itself out, I guess. I don't know. If need be, I'll talk to her myself. We didn't do anything wrong, Stu. We were free agents."

The truck pulls up alongside, and the driver reaches across to wind the passenger window down.

"Evening," Ida calls out to her.

Harper pushes a button and her driver's-side window slides down. "Hey, Ida. I was beginning to wonder if you'd show at all."

"Yeah, I got caught up."

"Uh-huh," Harper says. "Do you want to jump in back?"

Ida cuts the engine. "Okay," she says. Harper watches in the rearview mirror as Ida climbs in.

"Ida, this is Detective Stu Raley. He's my partner. You can trust him, okay?"

"I know," Ida says. "Pleasure to meet you."

Stu nods. "And you."

Harper starts the car, drives through the empty parking lot. She glances up at the mirror, sees Ida looking out the window at her truck. "It'll be fine there, Ida. I promise."

"Alright."

"Listen, I've told Stu about your . . . gift," Harper tells her. She feels Stu tense in the passenger seat.

Neither Ida nor Stu says anything.

"He's skeptical."

Stu glares at her. "Jane . . ."

"It's alright, Detective Raley," Ida says from behind. "I'm used to people thinking I'm a little soft in the head. Goes with the territory. I spent four years in a mental hospital because no one believed a word I was saying. You'll either be convinced, or you won't. I'm not out to impress anyone."

Stu clears his throat. "Uh, that's fine. Yeah."

Harper thinks: *So far so bad.*

Barnie watches the morgue overnight. The job involves him sitting at a desk watching television, trying to stay awake until the morning supervisor arrives. His proclivity for eating several bags of cheese balls every night, washed down with cans of Coke, has seen him balloon to a solid three hundred pounds.

Occasionally, people arrive at the morgue to deliver a body, or to take one away. It's Barnie's job to ensure everything is kosher. So when he sees Detectives Raley and Harper—and a third person he's never met before—approach the entrance, he's not too surprised. He knows they have that girl in storage, the one from the high-profile murder case that's all over the local paper. It's not unusual to have homicide people, and coroners, revisit a body to confirm some theory or other.

They ring the bell and he buzzes them in.

"Evening, Barnie," Raley says.

"Detective." He nods his head. "Harper, you along for the ride tonight?"

"I am."

Barnie peers around Harper's side at Ida. He lifts the sign-in sheet attached to a clipboard and sets it down on the counter in front of them. "Does your friend there have ID?"

"I'm afraid not," Raley says. "But you're due for a quick bathroom break, aren't you?"

Barnie stands up behind the desk and stretches for effect. "You know, I think I am. And I should walk the perimeter of the building to make sure there are no unsavory characters milling around. That should take ten minutes or so. Sign yourselves in while I'm gone?" He hands Raley a clipboard and a pen, then walks down the hall toward the restroom.

Stu follows Harper and Ida through the door.

Down a corridor, and through a door at the very end, Harper leads them into a room with chilled cabinets on either side. They have metal doors that open outward, revealing a sliding gurney. She locates the one for the latest victim, but pauses for a moment.

"Ida, are you okay so far?"

Ida gives her a sharp nod but doesn't speak. Harper wonders what she might be picking up on in there—what auras must surround the cold bodies in the walls.

She pulls the gurney out on its runners. The body is covered in a sheet. She peels it back to reveal the girl. Ashen faced now, a distinct blue tinge to her lips, her eyelids. Stu shifts uncomfortably as Ida approaches the body, extends her hand, and brings it to rest on the girl's icy skin. Her face tightens with revulsion, but she keeps her hand there, powering through the urge to recoil.

Harper moves back to stand with Stu, to give Ida space.

"I'm still not sure about this," Stu hisses in her ear. "If we're caught bringing her in here . . ."

Harper fixes him with a sharp look. "Not now."

Ida throws her head back, her whole body rigid, one hand on the girl's forehead, the other arm outstretched at an angle. A deep moan rises from her throat, as if she's being electrocuted. Stu goes to help her. Harper grabs his wrist. "No. Let her do this."

The already-low lighting in the room dims even more, and the temperature seems to jump up a few degrees.

The moan rises in pitch. It sounds as if Ida is in agony. "I can't . . . I don't believe this . . ."

Harper's grip tightens. *"Leave her."*

The connection is different. A living being has warmth, the reassuring rhythm of its heart, the flow of hot blood through miles of veins. It has the marriage of mind and spirit, united in forming a whole.

Ida relishes such connections. They bring insight, allow her to experience the bond of humanity she has missed out on. Tapping into memory, into feelings. Touching a pregnant woman's stomach, hearing the hum of the tiny life within . . . all of it a wonder.

With the dead, it's different.

It is not a merging of psyches, but an electric shock, a charge of energy fusing her to the spirit locked within the lifeless body. The voice howls like the wind: unbalanced, completely open. Pulling her in, forcing her to see, to hear, to feel . . .

Waking in a car. The door opening, getting pulled out under the armpits. It's dark.

Cold.

The dark sky is heavy with clouds and rain. Her feet drag in the wet earth. She is pulled back through rows of green, and when she is lowered to the ground, her senses come alive. She tries to scramble away, but he has her pinned. His face is a white mask; his eyes float in darkness. She tries to fight, to get loose.

He holds her, hits her. She can feel him wrestle with her underpants, tearing them apart in his fury. She tries to push him back; he hits her again. All she can do is grab at the mud, hold on to fistfuls of it as he breaks his way inside her, the pain radiating up her body despite the grogginess of whatever he injected her with.

Then his hands are around her throat. They are pressing; she pulls at his wrists, but they won't be moved. His arms are heavy steel, pushing down, crushing her. There is a throbbing light; it pulses, growing stronger, coming, going.

Ida knows this is her only chance.

What's your name? *she asks the girl in the last moments.* We don't know your name. We need to know.

Nothing comes. She is getting pulled back; the connection is coming apart, the fibers holding it in place breaking one by one.

Please. Tell me your name.

The darkness fades; the light creeps in around the edges like a false dawn and Ida hears a whisper. The last sound of the girl's soul. A final word.

"Gertie."

The lighting flickers above them. Ida is thrown back, stumbles on rubbery legs, and falls.

Stu rushes forward before Ida can crack the back of her head on the hard linoleum, catching her in his arms and lowering her slowly to the floor. Harper drops to her knees beside her and checks for a pulse.

"She's okay. Just out cold," she says. She looks up at Stu. "Now do you believe?"

"This could be an act," he says.

Harper taps Ida's face. There's no response, so she does it again, this time a bit harder, shaking her shoulders. Ida's eyes crack open, then try to close again. Harper shakes her. "Don't go back to sleep. Wake up."

"Huh?" Ida groans.

Harper looks at Stu. "Does this look like an act to you?"

"Could be. People fake being crazy all the time." He goes to say something else, rethinks it, gets to his feet instead. "I'll put the body away."

"How long have I been out?" Ida asks.

Harper smiles. "Seconds."

Ida groans again, rising to a sitting position. "Oh."

"What did you see?"

Ida tries to stand and almost doesn't make it before Harper scoops her under the arm and helps her up. Stu gets to her other side just in time.

"You're not going to be sick or anything, are you?" Stu asks her as they head for the door.

Ida shakes her head. "I just need air."

They steer her past the desk. Barnie is just returning from his patrol. "Jesus, is she okay?"

Stu waves him off. "She gets a bit funny around the dead."

Barnie rolls his eyes. "One of them, huh?"

Passing through the doors to the outside, they are hit by the cool night air. Ida inhales deeply, sucking it in, coming back to herself with each intake.

Harper and Stu let go of her arms and step back to give her space. Ida stands steady, but still looks diminished, as if she's been drained of energy.

She looks like someone who's just given birth, like everything's been sucked out of her.

"Ah, that's better. I feel like me now."

Harper asks her again: "What did you see?"

"He gave her something to make her sleepy. She tried to fight him off, but couldn't. She had dirt, in her hands. Squeezing it as he was . . . squeezing her. She could feel him doing his business, even as she was dying."

"Anything more? Could you see his car? What he looked like?"

Ida shakes her head. "She was too panicked to notice the car. He wore a hood, a white hood with the eyes cut out. And a belt around his neck. I got the impression he put it on after he kidnapped her. It scared her."

They walk to the car. Stu is the first to speak. "I have to look at the facts. That's what I believe in, what can be proved. You could be makin' this up."

"Stu—" Harper starts.

Ida shakes her head. "No, he's right. I don't blame him for not believing me. But there's one more thing. She gave me a name. Whether it's hers or not, I can't be sure. She said 'Gertie.'"

"Gertie," Stu repeats. "No second name?"

"No. That was it," Ida tells him. "Now, if that girl turns out to be a Gertie, or related to someone called Gertie . . . will you believe?"

Stu swallows.

Harper opens the door for Ida. "Let's get you back to your truck. You've still got a drive tonight. Or we can put you up in a motel if you don't feel up to it."

Stu looks at Harper. "Who's paying for *that*?"

Ida shakes her head. "I'm feeling okay now. I'll drive home. Never been much for motels. Dirty sheets and even dirtier bathtubs."

She climbs in. Harper shuts the door behind her. Stu is still standing there. "You okay?"

"I'm on the fence here," he says in a low voice.

"I figured as much. But she's right, Stu. If that name has any bearing, you have to believe her."

Stu looks down at the window, the outline of Ida's face there in the dark. "Or put her as a suspect," he says, walking around the front end to the passenger side. "Anyway, what does it matter what I believe? As long as the case gets solved, I don't give a fuck if tea leaves and chicken bones point us in the right direction. I just wanna bag this prick."

Harper watches him climb in, then gets in herself.

Ida gives them a wave from the cab of her truck and then heads out of the parking lot and onto the dark streets. She feels cold, as if she's back in the morgue, surrounded by the sleeping dead again.

Ida flexes her hand—she can still feel the icy kiss of the young woman's skin against hers, the charge of electrified particles that connected them both in those long, torturous moments. Ida runs the heater, turning the dial all the way to max. Soon warmth fills the truck, but she still feels the chill that inhabits her bones.

For a short while, we were connected. I felt the ice in her marrow. The awful agony of his hands around her throat, squeezing, squeezing, forcing her last breath away.

She turns on the radio, hoping that will take her mind off what she just experienced. Bobby Womack singing "Deep River" warbles through on the radio waves, semi-distorted as if it's beamed in from Mars.

Ida sings along to it, just to drown the voice in her head, the whisper of a broken soul saying a name, repeating it over and over and over and over.

"Gertie."

8

"You want a beer, Lester?"

He pulls up a chair at the kitchen table and sits down. "No, I got to drive."

"Coffee then."

"Okay," he says.

Ceeli called him over to her place on the pretense of another auto repair, but he can't find anything wrong with the vehicle. He knows the real reason she wanted him to come to her house.

"Mack not here today?" Lester asks her.

She rinses two cups. "Nope. He got work out of town. Won't be back till tomorrow night."

"Work hard," Lester notes.

"Sure does. Not that I see any of the money," Ceeli says, shaking her head.

Lester can hear someone walking on the flattened dry grass around the side of the house; then he sees Ceeli's neighbor cross the window. The back door is already open, but Julie knocks on the frame. "Yoo-hoo!"

"Ah, hi ya Julie honey," Ceeli says. "Want a coffee?"

"No thanks, Ceeli, I've gotta run." Her gaze falls to Lester, and for the briefest moment, she is unable to contain her expression, to keep the mask up. Revulsion flashes across her features; then it's gone, buried behind an exterior of mock acceptance. "Hey, Lester."

"Hello Julie."

"You headed out somewhere?" Ceeli asks her.

"Oh, yeah, heading into town. Wanted to know if you needed somethin'."

Ceeli shakes her head. "Don't think so."

"Well, alright then. You got my cell, you need anythin'," Julie says.

"I got your cell."

Julie nods at Lester. "Bye to you."

He smiles because he knows it repulses her. "Have a *nife* day!"

When Julie has gone, Ceeli breathes a sigh of relief and sags against the kitchen counter. "God, that woman gives me a headache. There's no getting rid of her."

She makes the coffee and tells Lester to go to the living room. Ceeli sets the cups on the coffee table as Lester throws himself down on the sofa.

She stands over him, pushes his head back, her finger under his chin so that he looks up at her. "You're the only joy I got in this world right now, Lester."

He swallows.

Ceeli straddles him, her big legs on either side of his, and kisses him. He can taste her bad breath, her cigarettes and coffee. The sleep that has covered her teeth in a gritty film she has yet to brush away. Pulling away from him, she sucks on his deformed top lip.

She reaches down, feels his limp dick through his jeans. She moves to the floor, kneeling before him, and sets about freeing his flaccid penis. His work bottoms gather at his feet.

"Honey," she says, her hands on his thighs, bending forward to lick his genitals, then the end of his prick. She stops and looks up at him. "Somethin' the matter baby?"

"Put it in your mouth."

"Soft like that?"

He stares at her, silent. Demanding. Ceeli holds his floppy dick and puts it in her mouth. Lester sits back, one hand on the table, the other on Ceeli's head, moving his fingers in her wiry black hair. He closes his eyes, thinks of the girl. In the field, in the rain. He was soaked through afterward, covered in mud. When he arranged her body, he'd wiped away the water that had collected in her eye sockets. Just thinking about her, about how he'd taken her among the rows of wet soybeans, is enough to get him hard. His cock throbs in Ceeli's mouth, and she instinctively works on it. Her tongue slides around his shaft, the tip of his dick. Lester pictures the girls, sees them in his mind, and it's enough to push him near the edge. He takes a handful of Ceeli's hair and forces her to take him farther down her throat. Thinking of the young woman in the rain. On top of her, between her legs, his hands around her throat as she looks at him, big bright eyes pleading with him.

Ceeli gags as Lester thrusts his hips forward, mercilessly fucking her mouth. All the while, his eyes are closed.

There is the girl, the smell of the damp earth, the rain coming down around them in the dark. Cold water running down his back, dripping off his twisted face. After, he went back to the car for his Polaroid and the crown, then returned to her. He placed the crown on her head and took pictures. Polaroids are like printing your own postcards, your own mementos of something you want to hold in your heart forever.

Lester opens his eyes.

The girls are still there.

The Hope and Ruin Coffee Bar is busy as usual, everyone jostling to keep their place in line. Harper's phone vibrates in her pocket. She checks it.

"Morelli," she tells Stu.

"Answer it, I'll get these."

"Thanks," she says, heading for the door to take the call outside. "Caramel latte."

Stu waves her off. "I know, kiddo."

Outside the heat is already cloying, the sultry air sticking to her skin. She swipes the phone and holds it to her ear. "Harper."

"Detective. Where you at?"

"I'm going to check in with Albie, see how he's doing with the dead girl's phone. We're still going through the files you gave me, trying to get what we can from them."

"Well, I have some good news. We've got a name to put with the girl," Morelli says.

"Really?"

"Yes. Gertie Wilson. Parents had her listed as missing last night. They went and identified her at the morgue a half hour ago. I've got Dudley bringing them in as we speak."

"Okay. Do you want us to come to the station?"

"No, you do what you're doing, and check in later. If you're okay with Dudley interviewing the parents, that is."

Harper grimaces. "I've got no issue. So long as he's tactful, sir."

"I'll have Clara O'Hare join him. You know Clara. She'll make sure he doesn't go too far."

"I appreciate that, Captain."

"What you said about Albie, he already got into the phone. Came up with the same name. Did it about an hour ago. He's getting into all the messages and call logs as we speak."

"Excellent."

"Oh, a heads-up—I'm going to hold a conference at the front of the station in the next hour. It might be best to avoid coming in until after then. Luckily, the files in your possession are the only copies left of the originals. The real records. The press will only be able to dig so far," Morelli says.

"Yes." Harper looks as the door to the coffee shop opens. Stu emerges, phone in the crook of his shoulder, carrying two coffees. She takes hers, freeing him up to hold his phone properly. She doesn't know who's on the other end of Stu's phone, but whoever it is has him riled up. His face is red, body language definitely aggressive.

"Uh, sir, about our conversation at the morgue—"

"Listen, Detective. You do what you've gotta do. I'll worry about my own ass. Check in with me later."

"I will, sir. I appreciate it."

The captain ends the call and Harper barely notices, her attention is so fixed on what Stu is doing. He paces back and forth, voice rising to near-hysterical levels as he gets angrier. Harper puts her phone away and walks toward him. Now she can hear his voice—an angry growl he doesn't make often. Only when he's really pissed.

". . . no, listen to me, Karen. No! You listen to me!"

Stu sees Harper coming and turns his back.

"Well I don't know where you got *that* from, but you're wrong. *So* fucking wrong . . . Who? He did? That's alright . . ."

He snaps his phone shut.

"Hey," Harper says.

"My ex-wife. She tells me I'm such a loser for cheating on her, for throwing my marriage away."

"Calm down. You look like you're about to have a stroke," Harper tells him in her most level, reasoning voice, despite the thumping of her own blood in her ears. "Let's go to the car."

"Wait. That's not it. Guess who bumped into her a while back in the supermarket, of all places?"

Harper draws a blank.

"Dudley. Karen said it was Dudley who told her about you and me, said we started hooking up as soon as we became partners. Told her we were having a fucking affair."

"What? she asks incredulously. "That little bastard . . . but why? That's so random."

"I don't know, but I'm gonna find out." Stu charges toward the car, his blood pressure up.

Harper catches up with him. "Stu, hold on a second. Don't go rushing off. Wait." She grabs him by the arm and forces him to stop. "Wait! Look, we don't know all the facts yet. But we will. It'll do us both no good to have you flying at Dudley right now. And anyway, we can't go to the station just yet."

"Why?"

"There's a ton of press there. Morelli told me to steer clear for now," Harper says.

Stu falls silent. He puts his coffee on the top of his car and leans against the side of the vehicle.

Harper uses a softer tone than usual. "Stu."

He looks at her.

"Why don't you come with me to see Ida? We can sort all this out later. I'll tell Morelli."

Stu considers it for a minute. Eventually he says, "Fine" and gets in the car.

Some of the time, they fuck all day.

Ceeli is fifty years old with a deep-brown, perfect complexion, has streaks of gray in her kinky black hair, but has kept a good figure. Her tits sag when they're free of her bra, but it doesn't bother Lester all that much—they're still big enough to bury his tortured face in when she's on top of him, and that's all that matters. He loves that she's skilled with those thick lips that are so quick to smile.

"You don't ever worry Mack *if* gonna find out?" Lester asks her, lying in the double bed she shares with her husband, watching Ceeli get back into her dress.

"No. He don't pay me no attention, Lester, you know that."

"Yeah."

"Besides," she says, grinning at him. "I like that big ole cock of yours. I swear, I never rode one like it. Makes me feel like a girl again."

He doesn't know what to say; he never does. The only time Lester is confident is when he's with his girls, when he makes them sleep, watching their faces change and knowing that they see him; they really see him for who he is inside. The angel in devil's clothing.

To Ceeli he is a toy to be played with. The role is reversed.

"What *waf* it you wanted fixin' anyway?" Lester asks, following Ceeli downstairs, adjusting the suspenders on his jeans.

"It was me needed the fixing, Lester honey. And God knows if you ain't done a good job this time," Ceeli says, followed by a hoarse chuckle. They walk into the kitchen. Ceeli holds a glass under the faucet at the sink.

Lester's hands fall to her hips, to the big round cheeks of her ass beneath the dress.

"Stop it, Lester. God, ain't you satisfied after screwin' me all day long? Damn, I can feel you're hard already."

She can't see the face he is making as he lifts the back of her skirt. "I'm never *fatiffied*."

Ceeli sighs with pleasure as his forefinger finds her slit, his free hand pressing her against the counter, the tap still running, spitting water everywhere.

"Go on, Lester. Go on," she urges him breathily. "I'm hurtin' but I'm achin'. Go on honey."

He quickly drops his jeans, runs his fingers across the folds of her vagina, feeling her wetness, her eagerness to have him inside her again. Ceeli reaches behind her, guides him in. "Oh God," she groans, leaning as far forward as she can. The water is spraying everywhere. "Honey . . ."

Julie carries her bag around the side of the house, eager to show Ceeli her finds. She snags one of the bags on an overgrown bush and curses as she tugs it free, continuing on. Julie looks through the window, at the point of announcing her presence when she freezes.

Lester, the dullard Ceeli has doing odd jobs at her place from time to time, is in the throes of fucking her neighbor over the sink. Julie shrinks back, not wanting to be seen, but filled with a dark desire to watch, all the same. She knows he could turn his head any second and see her standing there. But she's rooted to the spot.

Julie can hear Ceeli moan with pleasure, and she can hear Lester grunting with effort, his pale-white ass pushing in and out. The fronts of Ceeli's thighs slap against the cabinet as Lester pounds her so hard she cries out. Common sense kicks in and Julie backs off, retracing her steps and departing before she's noticed.

She hurries to her home, wanting to get out of sight while she decides what to do.

"Ass end of nowhere, ain't it?" Stu asks, getting out of the car and blinking in the sunlight.

Harper removes her shades. "Yeah, she likes her solitude."

"I'll say."

"Well, hello." Ida appears in the doorway. "You coming in? Or you want to sit outside?"

"Why don't we enjoy some of this sunshine?" Harper says, remembering how hot it was in the house.

They sit out on the porch, on chairs Ida pulls from around the side of the house. She offers them both a cool drink, but they decline.

"You come to talk about last night?"

"Yes, but there was something else, too. I wanted to know if you'd take a ride with me to Wisher's Pond."

Ida looks away, to the road where the heat creates a haze over the baked ground. "Figured as much. I knew it was only a matter of time."

"Are you willing to do it?" Harper asks her.

Ida looks at Stu. "Only if *he'll* do something first."

"Me?" Stu asks.

"Yeah," Ida says. "I can't help you two no further if you don't believe me. I've spent too long hiding my gift to have it doubted. There have been too many unbelievers in my life."

"What do you want?"

"Give me your hand, sugar," Ida tells him.

Reluctantly, he places his hand in hers. Ida closes her eyes. A minute stretches out, the two detectives all too aware of the sounds around them. The distant cars. Crickets in the grass. Somewhere far off, a crop duster's engine as it turns in the sky, leaving a trail of white smoke on the fields.

Then the sounds seem to fade. The air around them grows heavy.

Ida's eyes open slowly. Stu cannot look away from her big dark pupils. From the intensity of her glare. "Your daddy used to buy you those sherbets. Lemon ones. On the ride over, you bought yourself and Detective Harper a lemonade. The kind comes in a plastic cup with a lid, filled with crushed ice. Mint leaves on the top. You told her it reminded you of the sherbets your daddy used to buy."

Stu tries to move his hand, to pull it back, but Ida's grip tightens just enough to let him know she's serious, that he has to hear the rest.

"When he died, you found yourself walking through the town. You went into a little store there and got yourself a big old bag of those sherbets. Out in the park, there's a little river, and a bridge going over it. You sat on a bench near one side of that bridge, crying like you hadn't done in years, like a hurt child. All you could think about was your poor old man, six feet in the dirt. Everything you could've said to him, but didn't get a chance to."

"That's enough," Stu says. He tries to get his hand free, to move, to do something to break the spell, but he can't pull his hand from hers; he can't look away; he can't stop listening to her soft voice reveal the workings of his own heart.

Ida sighs. Her thumb works on the back of his hand, rubbing it gently, soothingly. A single tear rolls down her cheek, and Stu watches it fall to the porch, where it makes a puddle in the dust that covers the boards.

"You and your wife couldn't have kids. But you tried. God knows you wanted them kids, but they just wouldn't come. She blamed you. Little did she know just how much you wanted a kid all your own, to buy them lemon sherbets. To take on a long walk and tell 'em 'bout your daddy. Your missus never got that, sugar. She ain't never got that at all."

Ida lets go of his hand and he gets up, trying to get off the porch to hide his face, wet with tears. Harper starts to go after him but Ida shakes her head. "Let him have some space."

Stu stands with his back to them. The wind churns up from somewhere, blowing his tie out behind him.

"We got a name for the girl," Harper says, eyes still on Stu.

"I was right," Ida says. "Weren't I?"

"Yes."

She nods, her voice grave. "Like I said."

"Have you ever been to the scene of your mother's murder?"

"No."

"I thought it might stir something up, something new you might've forgotten from . . . well, you know . . ."

"Don't need no convincing. I'll do it," Ida says. "But don't be expecting some kind of revelation, sugar. In my experience, there's only what there is, and what there ain't."

◆ ◆ ◆

Stu is quiet on the drive to Wisher's Pond.

"It's a peaceful spot," Ida says, walking ahead of them. "The old-timers would come up here, snag catfish, and throw 'em back, just for sport. I don't think there's any catfish in there now, though. Probably eaten. Some folk got no respect for anything."

Harper looks at Stu. "You okay?" she whispers.

He nods. That's it. Ida is still talking. It doesn't sound like the spiel of a local tour guide, but the twittering of someone who is incredibly nervous, speaking just for the sake of doing so. They walk through the tall grass toward a cluster of trees in the middle of an abandoned field. On the drive over, Ida told them that no one had worked that land for a hundred years. "It's never dried up," she tells them. "Far as I'm aware. Always been here."

The trees are spaced out around the pond's edge, but far enough back from the bank to allow short, soft grass to grow there. Ida hesitates at the edge of the trees.

"You okay?" Stu asks Ida. It's the most he's spoken since leaving her house.

"Just cold."

Harper looks at Stu, and he shrugs to say he doesn't know what she's talking about either. It's extremely hot and sticky out. Stu removed his suit jacket and stripped off his tie back at the car. His shirt is undone a few buttons, revealing the vest beneath and the gathering of dark hairs on his chest. His sleeves are rolled up, as are Harper's.

"You feel cold?" Harper asks Ida.

She shakes her head. "No. I feel *the* cold," she says, walking slowly through the trees.

Ida picks her way around the old trunks, the strong smell of warm bark and the green pond water, the whisper of grass out in the field, pushed by a breath of hot air. She pauses, eyes closed, and it takes every inch of her resolve to continue. Coming up on the place she has revisited in her dreams since she was a little girl. Ida hunkers down on the ground, feeling the soil with her open hands, finding the spot where her mother died. Digging her fingers in, grabbing at the soil, clenching it, feeling it crushed in her hard grip, the grains, the coolness.

Here she lay. Here she died.

"Ida, is this the place?"

She nods.

"Damn . . . ," Stu says, looking around. "I remember the photos in the file now."

Harper squats down near Ida. "What're you feeling?"

"Just . . . she was here. *He* was here. Nothing specific—it's like turning a corner and seeing a building you used to look at as a kid," Ida says, looking about. "My mamma used to pour glasses of lemonade. Full of ice. The glass was so cold it'd sweat and drip everywhere. I think of that every time I see a cold glass. This place is like that. It's an echo. A memory."

"Anything more specific coming through?" Harper asks her.

Ida shakes her head. "No," she says, her face suddenly screwed up tight. Something sour in her mouth. "There's only pain here."

And fear.

Harper watches her get up. "Do you want to go home?"

"Yes," she says, hugging herself. "And I don't want to come back here ever again."

9

The sun is far behind the buildings on the other side of town when Harper and Stu arrive at the station. The press is reduced to a few men and women by now.

She stops the engine, and talks to him for a short while, warning him to hold his tongue around Dudley until they know all the facts. Even then, she tells him, he should go directly to Captain Morelli.

Stu clenches his jaw, looks dead ahead, and she can see his rage is at a simmer. Before walking inside, she stops him again.

"Promise me you won't go off."

Stu lets loose a big sigh. "Yeah."

"Stu?"

"Look, I said yes. Trust me. It'll be hard not to knock the little prick out, but I'll hold it back, okay?"

"Okay," Harper says, opening the station door and letting him go first. "You know you're hot when you're mad, though, right?"

He shrugs, playing along. "Sure do."

It must be fate, Harper thinks as Dudley approaches. Stu rubs his temple.

"Jane, I'll go do that thing," Stu says, heading straight for the basement.

"Okay. Check in with you later."

Dudley frowns, watching him go, but Stu's odd behavior is forgotten in Dudley's eager rush to impart his information.

He walks with Harper to her desk, where she sets down her bag and keys. "I interviewed Gertie Wilson's parents. They took it pretty hard. Said they listed her missing because it wasn't like her not to come home. She'd never done it before."

"Any boyfriends? Men hanging around?"

Dudley shakes his head. "None that they knew of. She was a good girl. Top student."

"What about Albie? Any luck with the records from the phone?"

Dudley nods. "He's in IT right now, pulling everything off of it. Should have it any minute. What I heard was he had the cell phone sitting in a bowl of rice to dry it out."

"Apparently that works," Harper says. "Did we get anywhere with the trucks in the local area?"

"Nope. There's just too many. Until we get a plate, or a distinguishing feature."

"I hear you," Harper says, looking at him—really looking—trying to determine if he's the sort who would do something like phone a colleague's ex-wife and cause trouble. He's hard to read. His appetite for the job, for career progression, his dickish behavior sometimes—it's possible.

"What's up with Detective Raley? He seemed off."

"Oh he's caught up in the case. Those young women, the way they've been killed. He's finding it tough switching off."

Dudley nods, as if he understands. "Yeah, I guess it gets that way, huh?"

"So anyway, I'll let you get going. I'll catch up with you later," she says.

Dudley flashes a smile—she notices again that the gesture does not fit his face. "Sure."

When she's certain he's gone for the time being, Harper heads down to the basement, where she finds Stu sitting at a table, the files in front of him.

"Stu? You okay?"

"Yeah," he says, as if nothing is wrong.

That's a bad sign, Harper thinks, but she tries to push the thought to the back of her head. He promised her he'd keep himself under control. She has to trust that's what's going to happen. "What're you looking at down here?"

"The files again. You know, we can't question the families of the other cases because they weren't made aware of the real circumstances. Their loved ones died, but they were lied to. Ida is our only link to the past, to this guy's first murder," Stu says. "But looking through them all, you see a definite pattern. He goes for the same look, the same build, the same kind of hair."

"Either he's revisiting that murder, over and over again, because he enjoyed it, or—"

Stu says, "He's infatuated. Something about Ida's mom, the way she looked. Do you think he had a thing for her?"

Harper shrugs. "Could've been what you were saying before, an infatuation. Does it say where Ruby worked?"

Stu leafs through the file, looks up, shaking his head. "No."

"I'll look into it. If he was an admirer, he might've been seen with her. People who worked with her might remember."

"It really kills me not being able to talk to the other families. We have this stack of files, but we're handicapped."

"I know. And I feel guilty, knowing the truth, knowing the pain they feel, and that they've been lied to all this time."

"But what can we do?"

"Nothing," Harper says. "Same way we can't go asking any of the other investigators. Claymore is our only lead, in that regard. The case will implode if those other guys catch wind of the truth being revealed. We can't have that yet."

"I know. It's shit."

"I'll dig around. We should check in with the captain soon. Say an hour or so?"

"Yeah."

She starts to leave and hears the chair scrape back from the table.

"Jane?"

Harper pauses at the door, turns back.

"Thanks for keeping my head cool," Stu tells her. "I would have done something I regretted otherwise."

"Anytime."

Albie moves aside as Harper pulls up a seat next to him. The IT room has a few officers working, a few of them chatting among themselves.

"So you got into it?"

He nods. "Yeah, it was impossible at first. The phone was water-logged, but a bowl of rice did the trick."

"That got it working?"

Albie shakes his head. "No. But it was enough to allow me to access its files, its data, and grab everything I could."

"Right. I'm with you."

Albie moves the cursor on the desktop to maximize a window that contains all of Gertie Wilson's incoming and outgoing calls. There are no names, just numbers, times, and dates. Next to that information is a time stamp indicating the duration of each call.

"Okay. So this is the call log," Harper says. "What about text messages?"

Albie shrinks the first window and maximizes another. "Ah, well, this is where it gets interesting. There are quite a few connected to different numbers. Friends, maybe her parents. But the interesting one is here . . ."

He shows Harper a seemingly unending series of exchanges, all from the same number. There's a name mentioned several times, too.

"Hugo," Harper says. "These messages read like boyfriend-girl-friend texts."

"They are," Albie says. "They're saying they love each other. Look."

Harper watches him highlight one text message in particular: "Love you" followed by a series of kisses and a smiley face.

Everyone loves an emoticon, Harper thinks.

"I take it you've already connected this Hugo to the number," she says.

Albie checks his notepad. "Hugo Escovado. I've got his address here."

"Good. First thing tomorrow, we're going out there," Harper tells him, getting up. "Get a patrol car to wait outside the house, monitor for movement, make sure he doesn't try to run. I'll pick you up from your apartment tomorrow morning at six."

"Okay, boss," Albie replies as she walks out of the room.

Mack slams his car door, cracking open a can of Bud and pouring it down his gullet as he crosses the street. If he were able to drink while driving, he would. As it is, he drives all the way home with a six-pack on the passenger seat. He's so thirsty for it he can almost taste it.

Some of the Bud runs down his chin and onto his already-stained work vest. Mack wipes his mouth on the back of his hand. He's a middle-aged white man with short Irish-red hair. His skin is red from the heat, his freckles and moles more pronounced the longer he spends under North Carolina's baking sun.

Julie walks across her front lawn. "Mack!" she calls, but not too loud, as if she's trying to avoid any undue attention from the rest of the street.

"Julie? How you doin'?"

"Oh, fine, fine. I gotta talk to you," she says, taking him by the arm and steering him toward her house. "Gotta talk to you in private."

She looks jittery, sounds like she's at the point of some kind of breakdown. Mack wrestles his arm free from her grip. "Damn, woman. What's got into you?"

Julie looks at him. "Mack, I saw something . . ." Tears fill her eyes.

"Julie, what's wrong? Someone done somethin' to you? Have you told Ceeli?"

Julie shakes her head. "No. This is *about* Ceeli, Mack. I saw her."

"Yeah?" he asks, smiling goofily. "Got new glasses, huh?"

She shakes her head, intent on what she wants to tell him. "Mack, that man Lester was at your house. I saw 'em through the window. They was doin' stuff in there." Julie buries her face in her hands. "I'm so sorry to tell you this, Mack. I saw 'em . . . together. I think Ceeli is havin' an affair."

Mack takes Julie by the shoulders, gives her a good shake. "Speak up and talk straight. Don't fucking flake out on me. What did you see 'em doin'?"

Julie trembles in his grip. "Having intercourse, Mack. I saw it. They was makin' love."

"That son of a bitch," he growls, pushing her away.

As Mack storms off her lawn and heads for his own house, Julie stumbles forward. "Please, Mack! Don't do anything stupid!"

He thunders through the front door, draining the beer and crushing the empty can in his fist before tossing it to one side on the floor. "Ceeli! Get your fuckin' ass out here!"

His wife appears at the top of the stairs, face tight. "Mack? What you shoutin' for?"

He points up at her. "I gotta talk with you, woman."

"Honey," she says, making her way down the stairs like a gazelle stepping out of the tall grass to take a drink of water, expecting a cheetah to leap at any moment. "I'm comin'."

"Quicker! God damn it, woman you'll be late to your own fuckin' funeral!" Mack screams, dragging her down the last few steps by her arm. Ceeli cries out as he whirls her around, then shoves her toward the kitchen. He scuffs his boot against her ass to provide added momentum. "Go on! Get!"

He hurries up behind her, gives her another push, sending her flying against the cupboard. "Mack, stop! What's this about? What's got into you?"

"No, Ceeli, it's who's got into you while my back's been turned, that's what."

She shakes her head, eyes wide. "Baby I don't know what you been told, but I ain't been up to nothin', I swear. Nothin'!"

Mack flicks his hand out, catches her in the mouth, splits her lip open. Ceeli's hand rushes to where she's been hit, the blood dribbling out from behind her fingers.

"Please, Mack . . . don't hurt me . . . ," she begs him, backing up against the stove. "I didn't mean nothin' by it, honey."

Mack jumps on her, punches her in the gut so hard she loses all the breath in her lungs and can't draw another. Ceeli gasps, drops to the cold kitchen tiles. Mack lifts her head by the hair, slaps her face.

She mumbles at his feet, sobbing, drawing ragged breaths. "Mack . . . please . . ."

He proceeds to punch her, left, right, left, right, her head swinging back and forth with each hit.

"It was that fuckin' moron, weren't it? I already know it," Mack growls, getting in her swollen face. "What did you do, eh, Ceeli? Did you suck his goddamn cock? Did you fuck him in our bed?"

Tears run from Ceeli's eyes, mixing with the blood on the side of her face. "I love you, Mack."

He stands upright, as if he's about to beat her again. That, or worse. But he doesn't strike her. Mack looks down at her as if she were no more than a bug crawling along the sidewalk. "I don't know you no more, woman. And let me make a promise to you. I'm goin' up to that freak's place and I'm gonna *end* that motherfucker!"

Julie comes running from her house at the sight of Mack walking back to his car, fists bloodied, his face red.

"Mack, what happened?" she asks him, getting near.

He rounds on her, shoves her back. She falls on her ass in the street. "Fuck off!" he shouts.

Julie scrambles away from him and Mack jumps in his car, the engine roaring to life. He sets off, tires screeching up the street. Julie waits for him to go, then looks at Ceeli's place.

What if she's dead in there?

She swallows, considers going in to check on her, but hesitates.

Why did I get involved? Why didn't I mind where I stuck my nose?

Her conscience wins and Julie goes to Ceeli's front door. She knocks on it and the door swings inward.

"Ceeli? You in?"

You know she is. He's probably smashed her head in and left her bleeding out . . .

"Ceeli?"

Julie finds her in the kitchen, lying on the tiles, trying to get herself to a sitting position. Her head is lumpy and swollen, the skin around both eyes rapidly turning black. There's a giant handprint across her face from where she's been hit.

"What you doin' here, Julie? Did you cause this?"

She shakes her head. "I didn't mean for any of—"

Ceeli suddenly bolts upright, snarling. "Get outta my house! Get out! GET OUT!"

Any thoughts Julie had of calling an ambulance, or the police, are forgotten as she runs from Ceeli's house, crying.

Why did I open my big fat mouth?

Stu raps his fingertips on the edge of her desk. "You ready?"

Harper gets up. "Yeah—" She catches a blonde-haired woman walking into the office, scanning the room at first, then spotting them. "Oh fuck."

Stu frowns. "What?"

Harper nods in the direction of his ex-wife, headed their way. "Trouble."

He turns around, with Karen in his face within seconds. She shoves him in the chest, knocking his butt against the desk.

"What the fuck, Karen?"

Harper starts to move in on her, grab her in a headlock, and slam her down on the desk, but Stu gets in the way. "Stu—"

"I'll handle this."

Harper glances about—it's no surprise everyone has stopped what they're doing to watch the drama unfold. In her peripheral vision she can see Dudley hovering nervously, unsure what to do.

"You cheating bastard. What, you thought I wouldn't find out, you son of a bitch?" Karen looks around him, eyes lighting on Harper. "This your new girlfriend?"

Harper comes around the desk, hands open in front of her in the most disarming gesture she can muster. "Karen, please calm down. There's a time and place—"

Karen lunges for her. Stu is able to hold Karen back, but not before she reaches Harper's hair. She pulls hard. Harper stumbles forward, regains her footing, holds her hair to prevent Karen from ripping it clean out. "Get her off!"

"I'm *trying*!" Stu yells. He's grappling her around the waist, pulling her back, but Karen isn't letting go. What's more, she's started to kick. Harper leans back, snarling at the pain, barely avoiding Karen's shoe.

"Fuckin' whore!"

Harper reaches up for Karen's face, the side of her head, and then her hair. She grabs a big handful of it and tries to pull it from her head. Karen cries out in pain, which only makes her harden her grip. Stu inserts himself between them, and officers pile in, pulling the two women back from one another.

"I don't know what you've been told," Harper gasps, "but it's bullshit."

"You slept with my man, then he left me. It's pretty simple!" Karen starts forward again, straining against the arms and hands holding her in place.

Captain Morelli's voice booms across the office.

"WHAT THE HELL IS GOING ON HERE!?"

Lester is eating cold spaghetti rings from the can with a fork.

He sits in his shorts, flicking his hand at the flies buzzing around his dinner. The TV booms out—an old black-and-white western he's seen a dozen times before. He digs into the can, watching the screen, and almost shovels the spaghetti rings in without looking. But he stops, noticing that a big black fly has settled on the fork. It sits staring back at him, as if trying to determine what he is.

You gotta eat it all lester or no puddin'...

Lester opens his mouth, rams the fork in, then clamps his tortured lips around it as he pulls it out. He has a mouthful of cold, slimy spaghetti rings and a juicy black fly trying desperately to get out. It buzzes against his cheek, rolls around his teeth, filling his mouth with its panic. Lester bites down hard, mushing the spaghetti rings together, missing the fly. He chews, misses it again.

He waits, clamps his jaws down. His teeth crunch on the fly, and he can taste it with the chemical-tainted tomato sauce the spaghetti is canned in. A few chews and he swallows the whole concoction, amused with himself, secretly hoping it'll happen again someday.

See i knew you could do it what a big boy you are . . .

He grins stupidly to himself. "Thank*f*, Mama," he says to the empty house.

The phone rings. Lester growls, throws the can down on the table, and storms over to the phone.

"Yeah?" he spits into the receiver.

"Lester . . . it's Ceeli."

"*F*eeli?" he asks, frowning.

She's crying. "He's coming for you, Lester. Mack knows. He's coming up there. He knows everythin'. You've gotta—"

Lester slams the phone back in its cradle and heads for his bedroom.

Mack stops the car, looks up at the house on the hill. It reminds him of the summer night back when he was a teen, taking Christine Fogelhorn to the Hope's Peak Cinema to see a midnight screening of *Psycho*. She worked at the diner and he'd been chatting her up for weeks, working his way toward asking her out. To his surprise she agreed.

They made out during the film, and he only caught glimpses of the movie in between getting his hand up her shirt, but he remembers the house. The weird, twisted way it seemed to jut from the landscape. As if the earth had spewed it out as something unwholesome.

Lester Simmons's place is like that.

Mack goes to the trunk and retrieves the metal baseball bat he keeps there in case he finds himself in an unfavorable situation. He locks the car, wipes his nose on the back of his hand, and catches a glimpse of his knuckles as he does—the skin broken, fresh blood in the cracks. He wonders how Ceeli's face looks. He wonders how he'll explain it away if she calls the cops, and realizes he doesn't give a shit.

There's only one thing on his mind. Getting to Lester and giving him a good beating. Maybe smashing his balls so hard with the bat they swell and the doctors have to take them off.

Lester's old truck is parked out front. He has all sorts of junk covering the backseat, but the front is clear. Mack goes to the house and is about to ring the doorbell when a thought occurs to him: *Why announce yourself? Go in the back. Surprise the bastard.*

Mack unlatches a gate and edges around the side of the house, holding the bat away from himself so that he can swing it at a moment's notice. The backyard is a wild, overgrown tangle. There are rusted trash cans to his right, a similarly rusted set of swings to his left.

Must be from when the ugly little freak was a kid.

Ahead of him, the long, dry grass grows haphazardly. Crickets chirp all around him. The back of the yard is uneven; there is an old shed there, half rotten, its door open. Mack approaches it, wondering if Lester is in there. He holds the bat at the ready and peers around the open doorway. The dusty sunlight falls on one side of the shed. The wall in front of him is covered in newspaper clippings pasted to the wood. It has peeled, faded, and rotted away in places. Polaroids tacked to the wood among the clippings show black girls asleep. Mack cocks his head to one side, walking into the shed to get a better look. He pulls one of the Polaroids free. It's pretty sun faded, but he can make out the girl's face.

She isn't asleep. *She's dead.*

"What the—"

A creak behind him. Mack spins around. A tall, gangly man stands in the doorway wearing only his shorts. His head is covered in a white sheet. There is a brown leather belt around his neck, holding the sheet tight. The man looks out through two warped eyeholes, every breath sucking the material in and out, in and out.

Mack hesitates.

That's all it takes.

◆ ◆ ◆

Why do I feel like a little kid who's been sent to the principal's office?

"Okay. Let's go over this again," Morelli says, rubbing his temple. The man looks tired, drained. Harper feels guilty piling more pressure on him. "From the top."

Stu leans forward. At some point, Karen must have smashed him in the face—he has a healthy shiner coming up, making his right eye swell. "Captain, I broke up with Karen, filed for divorce. It was all aboveboard. There was no affair."

"And you, Jane? You've been seeing Raley since then?"

"A while after, yeah," Harper says. "And we're not really seeing each other, sir."

Stu gives her a look that says: *Are you kidding me?*

Morelli frowns. "Then just what are you two?"

"I don't know, sir," Harper says.

"Well, you'd better decide. I can't have whatever is going on between the pair of you getting brought into this office. Especially now, with—"

Kapersky doesn't knock on the captain's door; she just throws it open. "Captain, you need to see this," she says, bounding over to the television.

"What the hell, Kapersky? We're in the middle of something here!"

The TV comes on, showing the front of the police station. The reporters are talking to a woman with blonde hair. She is sobbing into the camera, pouring her heart out. It's Karen.

Harper looks at Stu. He has his head in his hands, as if he's about to break.

"I don't believe this!" Morelli yells. Kapersky hurries from the office, closing the door behind her. The captain glares at Stu. "Hold your fucking head up! I knew I should've booked that crazy bitch. But out of deference to you, I cut her loose."

"Sir—"

Morelli groans, pacing back and forth in the narrow space behind his desk. "Shit! This is just what I need. Something else for these blood-suckers to latch on to."

Harper looks at the TV, feels her heart sink at the sight of Stu's ex.

The captain shakes his head wearily, looking all the more as if he has the weight of the world resting upon his shoulders. "This bullshit with your ex can't be seen to be getting in the way of this investigation. So, as of now, Raley, I don't want you within shouting distance of this case. I can't have you in the public eye, not like this. For all intents and purposes, you're suspended with pay until this has passed. As for you, Harper, I want you to take a few days off. Cool the fuck down. The investigation comes first, Detectives, not your love life."

"Sir! You can't expect me to stop working on this case," Harper tells him, the wind knocked out of her.

Morelli looks at her. "Who said anything about doing that? I'm saying I don't want to see you in this station for forty-eight hours. Understand?"

"Captain!" Stu stands and Harper knows what's coming. "Dudley—"

"Is a competent detective," Harper cuts in. Stu looks at her, unsure of what she's doing. "More than capable of continuing the investigation."

Morelli frowns as he regards the both of them. "I don't appreciate the personal lives of my detectives disrupting an ongoing investigation. Especially a high-profile one like this is turning into. Or the drama you've brought into my station. I don't know what's going on with you two, but I want you to sort your shit out."

"We will."

"Great. Now will the both of you please get the fuck out of here?"

Stu shakes his head as they walk away from Morelli's office, everyone watching them, neither of them caring about the looks they're getting.

"I don't understand you," he says.

Harper scans the office, spots Dudley over in a corner, on the phone. "I didn't think you would. Look, go grab what we need. Slip out the back, okay? I'll pick you up from there so the reporters don't see you coming and add more fuel to the fire."

"What're you gonna do?"

She doesn't answer him, just heads for John Dudley, aware of how disheveled she looks, how she has been humiliated in front of all her colleagues, and really not caring. She glances back to make sure Stu hasn't followed her. He hasn't.

"Dudley?"

He turns the phone away. "Yes, Jane?"

"Can I have a word?"

His tongue flicks out over his top lip, lizardlike. "Sure," he says, voice not so cocksure as usual. Harper leads him to one of the interview rooms and shuts the door. "What's this about?"

"You know what the hell this is about, John," Harper says, hands on her hips. "It's about you telling Stu's ex-wife that we were having an affair when we weren't."

Dudley doesn't even try to deny it. His tongue flicks out again. "Look, I didn't mean it like that. I bumped into her, we got to talking—"

Harper slaps him in the face. Dudley recoils, his hand to his cheek. "Christ! What was that for?"

She jabs him in the chest. "Interfere in my personal business again, I'll make it my purpose in life to fuck you, alright?"

"Y-y-yes," he stammers, blood rushing to his head.

She opens the door and looks back at him. "Why did you do it? What made you start this, John? Is this some kind of joke to you?"

Dudley can't maintain eye contact with her. He has to look away, look down at the floor, one hand clamped to the side of his face. Harper already feels a pang of guilt for hitting him so hard.

"I saw you with Raley and . . . I suppose I thought . . . we . . ."

Harper looks him up and down. "You're pathetic," she says, slamming the door behind her.

Lester has Mack down on the ground, hands around his throat, squeezing so hard his fingers almost break the flesh. Mack's last gargled breaths come sputtering out, his eyes bulging. Lester smiles behind the mask. The release is the same as when he takes the life from his girls. When he sees the light drain from their eyes, sees it dwindle to nothing, it's the biggest thrill he's ever known. A sense of greatness. The power of his own hands, bringing death, ending their journey.

But it's not the only thing that's the same. His cock is stiff in his shorts, throbbing against the constricting material, aching to be let free.

That there is a man . . .

Lester loosens his grip on Mack's throat. Now he's not sure.

You gettin' hard for a man are you turned on?

He lets go altogether. Mack gasps for breath, coughing and spluttering as Lester rolls off him.

If you get a hard-on from a man then you're one of them queers! *What will people think if you're one of* them, *huh? Remember what i said about queers?*

Mack thinks he has a chance. He thinks Lester will let him go.

"No!"

Lester stands, drags Mack out to the yard. He looks around. He sees the swing set. He hauls him over to it, grabs Mack's head in both hands, and screams as he proceeds to bash Mack's head against the rusted metal. The sound hurtling out of Lester's mouth is guttural, primal, from someplace deep inside. He breaks Mack's skull open, continues to crash his head against the frame of the swing until there are brains and blood. Until Mack's legs have stopped kicking.

Lester screams like a savage long after he is finished. When the scream has died in his throat, he reaches down to rub his softening cock. Lester feels wet, examines his fingers, and finds them covered in sticky semen.

He holds his hands out in front of him and they're shaking.

10

"Come in," Stu tells Harper, unlocking his door. "Let me pour you a drink or something."

Harper thinks about it and is about to tell him no, she should really get back, when she finds herself saying the complete opposite. *Why not? It's been a shitty kind of day. I mean, could this day get any worse?*

"Alright."

Stu smiles. "Good. I've got Glenfiddich."

"Even better, then."

Up in Stu's apartment, Harper flops onto his sofa as he fixes the drinks. Neat, no ice, no mixer. He hands her the glass, clinking his against hers. "Cheers."

"Cheers." Harper knocks it back, feels its velvet smoothness in her gullet, the burn as it reaches her insides and the ensuing warmth throughout. "God, that hit the spot."

"Another?" he asks, draining his glass in the same fashion.

"Please."

Harper runs her fingers through her hair, kicks her shoes off.

"Here you go," he says, handing her back the glass. "What a shitty day."

"Tell me about it. What're you going to do about Karen?"

Stu thinks for a moment. "Let it blow over. There's no more point talking to her. I'll change my number. That way she's got no way to contact me. She sure as hell won't come to the station again. We've got no ties, she's got no reason to call me anymore, huh?"

"Other than to give you shit, you mean."

He laughs. "Yeah, something like that. Anyway, how's the hair? You're the one who got roughed up today."

"I take it you haven't seen the massive shiner you got."

"Really?" Stu gets up and finds a mirror. "Ah, damn. That's a beauty."

Harper shakes her head, laughing, lifting the glass to her lips. "I confronted Dudley."

"What? That was my job!"

She puts a hand on his knee. "Calm down. It's all out in the open. He did it because he was jealous of us."

"You mean he's got a thing for you?"

"Uh-huh. That's why he did it. I don't think he expected it to go down the way it did at the station, though," Harper says. "I'll be interested to see what he does now. Whether he stays and tries to work it out, or gets a transfer."

"Hopefully the latter," Stu says, drinking his scotch.

"He's just a mean little man." Harper reaches up, rests her palm against the side of his face. "Stud. Your poor eye."

"It's nothing."

Whether it's the scotch, the emotion that rides in on the wake of a trauma, or just a case of perfect timing, Harper finds herself sitting up, leaning forward. Stu leans into her, his hand going to her waist, everything else forgotten. They kiss, softly at first, then with their lips pressed hard against one another, teeth clashing, tongues exploring, teasing, playing. His hand rides up her shirt, finds her breast, gives it a firm squeeze. Harper traces her fingers down his chest, to his leg, to his groin.

"You're sure?" Stu asks her, pulling away.

"I need this," she tells him between heavy breaths, looking deep into his eyes, pulling him back in, wanting him to take her, wanting to *feel* wanted. If for only the night, she wants all of that.

She wants to forget.

Ida lights a couple of candles, then holds the end of her cigarette to one of the flickering flames. The cigarette smoldering between her pursed lips, she flips through her record collection, letting fate decide.

She smiles when she pulls *Blonde on Blonde*—long one of her favorites—from the stack. She jumps in with "I Want You," swaying her hips back and forth to the freewheeling rhythm. She cracks open a cold beer, drinking and smoking as she slow dances around the house. Ida is caught up in the music, in her own thoughts, in the feelings Dylan always manages to expose.

Her favorite comes last, and it makes her more contemplative: "Sad-Eyed Lady of the Lowlands."

I am that sad-eyed lady, Ida thinks, finishing her beer, thinking that maybe she's had too many, but that maybe it's okay. She should have another. Drink until she sleeps.

Maybe the dream won't come, then.

Ida sits on her sofa, sets what's left of her cigarette on the edge of the ashtray, and buries her face in her hands. What she felt, visiting the spot where her mother died, has lingered. It was an aching loss, a knowledge of something terrible. She felt what her mother felt, the crushing, desperate panic.

She begins to sob, listening to Dylan's drawl, the tragedy of the musical arrangement, her ragged breath coming between waves of her grief. *Blonde on Blonde* comes to an end, the needle arm lifting from the vinyl, the turntable stopping dead, but the speakers still crackling, waiting for their next song. Their next voice.

An old poem surfaces in her mind. Something by Robert Frost she remembers from when she was a teenager:

One can see what will trouble
This sleep of mine, whatever sleep it is.

She has spent her entire life waiting to see what will trouble her dreams. Ida slips *Blonde on Blonde* back in its sleeve and busies herself picking something else. She's in no hurry to sleep.

Lester has put the mask and belt back in their special place—the stiff white cotton folded the exact same way he always does, shown the respect it deserves. The belt held in his hand, gripping the buckle, then coiling the leather tight around his fist. He put them in the drawer, in the cabinet next to his bed, as he always did.

He tips his head back, drains the last of a beer, then tosses the empty can out across the grass. There's something fitting about toasting Mack's body with his own beer. The flies have gathered on his corpse—they cluster around the opening in his skull. It's like a yawning mouth in the middle of all that white scalp and short, bristly, red hair. The brain matter that sticks to the swing set has already started to dry.

Lester looks at the old trash cans. The remains will never fit in one as he is. Lester goes into the house, where he keeps the log-splitting axe next to the fridge. He walks toward Mack's body, swinging the axe back and forth, hefting its weight in his hands. Best to remove Mack's legs and arms, then cut his torso in two. That way he can stuff him into one of the cans, and keep the fire contained to one cylinder.

"*Forry*, Mack," he spits, lifting the axe high. The blade flashes in the fading light, and he brings it down with a heavy chomping sound.

When he's done, Lester wipes the blood splatter from his mouth and fetches one of the rusted old trash cans. He drags it across the grass, sets it just right, then piles Mack's body parts inside. His head sits on the top, like a cherry on a cake. A liberal soaking with gasoline, and Lester lights a match, tossing it in and stepping back. The flames roar, consuming Mack's head, melting it away. It reminds Lester of a hog roast he once watched on TV. The fat popped and hissed as the hog turned on the spit, the same way Mack does now. When all is said and done, and the fire has died away, he will collect the charred bones and teeth and bury them.

The air is filled with cloying smoke and the stink of burnt pork, but Lester watches the fire dance long after the stars have come out. He doesn't know how he got to be so clever.

Harper lies stretched out on Stu's bed, one leg over his, listening to his breathing as he sleeps. There's a thin sheet across them—it's too hot in his apartment to sleep with anything heavier. The fan turns on the ceiling, chomping at the warm air.

She tries to get a fix on what's going to happen with her and Stu. Was tonight one last fling? Or was it the beginning of a continuation? Harper closes her eyes, tries to switch off, but she can't. The last thing she wanted to do was get into another full-on relationship. Leaving San Francisco, she'd been happy to call it a day on men for a while. Let her marriage shrink in the distance before she started looking forward to whatever was next.

But I didn't count on meeting a guy like Stu.

Deep down he is a good person, a caring individual who's been through the wringer just as she has. It helps that he's good-looking, too. In a way, they'd needed each other.

Is that all it is? A relationship born of convenience?

Harper looks at him, at his chest rising and falling, at the shadow of the fan intermittently revealing his face and suspending it in shadow in the space of seconds.

No. This is more. We were meant to get together.

Morelli tasked them with getting their heads right, and she knows that none of this will help. It'll only make matters more complicated. She'd been determined to cool it off between herself and Stu.

Lasted long, didn't it?

Harper gets up, careful not to wake him, and hunts for her clothes. The clock says 2:00 a.m. She has to get out of there, get to her own place. Dressing in the dark, she looks at Stu and feels her stomach flutter, not only at the sight of him, but at the prospect of being with him. In that moment, Harper almost stays.

But before she can rethink it, she's out in the street, unlocking her car.

There was no sleep to be found. Harper stops outside Albie's apartment complex, and he climbs into the passenger seat.

"Morning."

It's already light at six in the morning, and Harper has her shades on. "I guess it is."

Albie looks behind him. "No Stu?"

"Afraid not," Harper says, putting the car into gear and starting off. "Stu Raley is otherwise indisposed. We'll shoot over, just the two of us."

"Okay. And if the captain asks?" Albie asks her.

"I don't know." Harper shrugs. "Tell him to kiss your ass?"

"Thanks. Big help." Albie runs a hand over his face. "Listen, Harper . . . is this, like, off the record?"

"No, we arranged this yesterday."

He shifts in his seat. "Yeah, I know that. But that was before the Queen Bitch from Satan's Armpit came in the station and pulled half your scalp out."

"Don't sweat it, Albie."

"I'm not. I'm not. Believe me. But word is Morelli suspended you," he says. She can hear the uncertainty, the nervousness in his voice.

Harper glances sidelong at him. "It's only half true. I'm still on the case. It's all complicated, Albie. Just trust me. Nothing will fall on you."

"Okay, if you say so."

Twenty minutes later, they arrive at the residence of Hugo Escovado. Harper sits with her hands on the steering wheel, regarding the house through the windshield.

Across the road is the patrol car. "Come on, let's get this done," she says, climbing out.

She crosses the street, Albie in tow. The two male officers in the black-and-white get out and stretch.

"Ah! If it isn't Weinberg and Tasker."

Weinberg tips his hat. "Morning, Detective."

She looks at his partner, on the other side of the car. "Feeling better now, Tasker?"

"Almost," he says, embarrassed.

"Where d'you want us?" Weinberg asks her.

Harper thumbs in the direction of the house. "We're going in there to talk to a suspect. I want you two fine gentlemen to wait at the door. If you hear me shout, one goes in the front door. The other goes round back."

"Got it. You're the boss," Weinberg says.

Harper looks at Albie. "Don't you say anything."

"Was I about to?"

Esmerelda Escovado stands to one side and tells them to go on through to the living room.

Harper notices the pictures on the walls. Hugo, his parents, and what looks like a younger sister.

"I'll just go wake him. He's still asleep," Esmerelda says. "Please, sit down. I won't be a minute."

Harper smiles. "Thank you."

There are two sofas and a chair. Albie sits in the chair, and Harper sits on the sofa to the right. When Hugo and his mother come downstairs, they will intuitively choose to sit on the middle sofa, as it's unoccupied—when you board a bus or train, you hunt for two free seats together. You don't just sit right next to a stranger . . . unless that's your thing, of course.

"Detectives, this is my son, Hugo," Esmerelda says.

Hugo enters the living room sheepishly. "Uh . . . hi."

Harper nods. "Morning, Hugo. Please, take a seat. I am Detective Jane Harper. That there is Detective Albie Goode. We're with Hope's Peak PD."

Hugo has turned a definite shade of white. He sits down and his mother perches next to him. "Is my son in trouble?"

"Not right now," Harper says. "Hugo, we're investigating a very serious crime."

The kid swallows. "Okay."

"When was the last time you spoke to Gertie Wilson?" Harper asks him.

Realization dawns on his face. He sits forward, eyes wide. "Gertie? Has something happened to Gertie?"

Harper waves him back. "Slow it down a notch. When was the last time you spoke to her?"

"About three days ago, I guess."

"Where's your phone?"

He digs into his sweatpants pocket for his cell phone, swipes the screen, and hands it to her. Harper walks across the room and gives it to Albie.

She stands in front of Esmerelda and Hugo. "I've been led to believe you and Gertie were going out?"

"Yes."

Esmerelda looks at him. "Really? I thought you were just friends."

Hugo shakes his head. "No, Mom. I didn't want to say anything because, well, you know. Her being black and all."

"Oh, Hugo! You know I am not a racist!"

He puts her hands in his. "Mom, I didn't know how you'd react. You and Pop are pretty old-fashioned with a lot of things."

Esmerelda's face flushes red. "I'm very angry. Really, I am," she says, looking up at Harper. "We came here from Mexico thirty years ago, as immigrants. We have sought acceptance from black, white, Asian . . . We are all Americans. I never gave my son any indication I would frown upon such a pairing."

Before Harper can reply, Hugo is on point. "I know, Mom, but Maria Torres down the street introduced her black boyfriend to her parents. Half an hour later her Dad's getting hauled downtown by the police for threatening behavior."

"Well, I can assure you *that* will never happen here," Esmerelda says.

A big coffee table sits atop a white rug in the middle of the room. Harper perches on the edge of it so she can look them both in the eye.

"We found Gertie's body left in a crop field just outside of town. It's taken all this time to get into her phone and retrieve her call logs and her messages," she says, looking squarely at Hugo.

"She . . . you found her . . . what?" Hugo mumbles, shaking his head. "It can't be true."

"I'm afraid it is, son," Harper assures him. "I'm sorry, but I have to ask this. I need to know where you were three days ago, Hugo. Her last message to you was at four thirty in the afternoon. I need to know where you were from four thirty, till the following morning."

Without hesitation, Esmerelda says, "He was here with us. We ate out at Lorenzo's in town, had pizza, then we went and watched a movie as a family."

"Uh-huh." Harper glances at Albie. "How're you doing with that?"

He shrugs. "It's all here," he says, handing it to Hugo, then sitting back down.

"Okay," Harper says. "I'm going to need to see some kind of receipt. And maybe ticket stubs for the movie theater if you have them."

Esmerelda is instantly on her feet. "I keep all that stuff. I'll go get them."

Hugo is very quiet. He's watching the floor, lost in his own thoughts.

"Hey," Harper says in a soft voice, sitting next to him. "Are you okay?"

"Gertie's . . . gone?"

"I'm afraid so."

A single tear rolls down the boy's cheek and falls into his lap. "I can't believe it."

Harper feels her heart sink. There's no way this boy—this kid— killed Gertie. He loved her. She can see it.

"I'm so sorry, Hugo."

Esmerelda returns with the receipts and stubs, just as Harper asked. It clearly says three medium pizzas, four Cokes, and four sundaes on the receipt for Lorenzo's . . . unless Esmerelda's husband and daughter are exceptionally large and have voracious appetites, then Hugo was with them.

Harper looks at the stubs. There are indeed four of them, with the ticket price, the time, and screen in the top corner. She gets up to let Esmerelda return to her son's side and watches as she throws her arm around him.

"Oh, Hugo . . . ," she whispers, kissing the top of his head as if he is a child again.

Harper turns to Albie. "Hey, uh, go tell those two they can head off now. Why don't you go wait by the car. I won't be a minute."

"Sure."

"Listen, Hugo . . . there may be further questions at some point. But for now, your alibi checks out. Look, I can tell you cared for Gertie. And I want you to know I'm doing everything I can to get to the bottom of this."

Hugo looks up, eyes red. "Will that bring her back?"

Harper is stuck for what to say. His face, his words, the pain—they hit her right in the chest.

"No it won't. But it might let her rest," she says, excusing herself and stepping outside. It's a bright, hot day. Once more she finds herself missing the Bay Area, the cool mist, the smell of the salt water. She can still smell the ocean in Hope's Peak, but it doesn't compare with what she could smell in San Francisco. Harper slips her shades on and walks to the car.

She drops Albie back at his complex so that he can collect his car and warns him not to tell anyone other than Morelli.

"Of course. I'm on your side, remember, boss?"

Harper watches him go, then hits the road. For a moment, she considers calling Stu, but decides against it. She wants to be alone right now. To drive her car in solitude, except for maybe her thoughts.

And they are not quiet.

It's ten in the morning and music pours from Ida's house. Harper knocks on the door frame, but gets no answer.

"Ida?" she calls, easing the screen door open. There's a Jimi Hendrix LP on the turntable, its sleeve propped next to it. "Ida?"

Ida appears in the kitchen doorway, apron on, flour on her hands. "Harper? You gave me a scare."

"Sorry. I got no answer at the door."

"It's okay. I like it loud. Here, come in the kitchen," Ida tells her. "Do you want tea? I was about to have some."

"Yes, please," Harper says.

The kitchen is old, but clean. Lived in, some would say. Harper takes a seat at a little table with two chairs. There's a ficus tree in the middle—perhaps the biggest she's ever seen.

Ida nods in her direction. "Was my grandmammy's. She had it from a little girl."

"Really? It's very big."

"She lost it once. Grew it for ages, and lost it. All she had left was a single leaf," Ida tells her, filling the kettle and putting it on the stove to heat. "But you know, if you plant that one leaf in soil, it'll grow. Like the old saying. From small things, big things someday come."

Ida sets a ceramic teapot on the counter, puts three teabags inside, then rinses out a pair of cups.

"So this whole plant is from that leaf," Harper says. "Amazing, isn't it?"

"Milk and sugar?"

"Just as it is, please," Harper says. "And from now on, how about just Jane?"

"Okay, Jane." Ida hands her a cup. "Is that alright?"

"Perfect." Harper listens to the music. "Have you always been into music?"

Ida sits opposite her. "Since getting out of the hospital. My mother would always play her records when she finished work. It's one of the clearest memories I have of her. Diana Ross, Gladys Knight, Nina Simone, you know, all those old names. When she passed, and I ended up in the hospital, I missed hearing those songs."

"You were in there for what, four years?"

"Yes. It was after finding my grandfather the way I did. I came out just in time for my grandmammy to leave as well."

"That must've been awful."

Ida looks at her tea. "It was. Still is. But I moved on. She wanted to die at home, but they wouldn't let her, so they put her in the hospice."

"Sorry to ask, but what did she die from?"

"They said it was cancer of the stomach," Ida tells her. "But by the end, it was everywhere."

Harper lifts her tea, takes a sip. "I'll bet that was hard to deal with."

"No, actually," Ida says, smiling lightly. "It was beautiful."

"I don't follow," Harper says, frowning.

Ida takes a deep breath. "She fell into a coma near the end, and I'd sit up at that hospice holding her hand. The whole time, all I got from her was good things. Memories, moments. Sunny days. All the light of her life, do you know what I mean, Jane?"

"I think so."

"Then, toward the end, that's all there was—light." She looks up, eyes glistening. "That's what awaits most of us, Jane. Warm sunlight from that other place. It just gets brighter and brighter until there's nothing else."

"You've seen this?" Harper asks, her voice barely a whisper.

Ida nods slowly. "I've never forgotten it. The kiss of that sun is like nothing I've ever felt."

"What about bad people, Ida? What's in store for them?"

Ida's lips press to a thin line, her jaw taut as she sets her cup down on the table. "What they deserve, Jane."

A timer goes off in the kitchen, and Ida moves to a metal mixing bowl on the windowsill, peels back a dish towel to reveal dough risen almost to the surface. Harper watches as Ida slaps the dough with the back of her hand, and it sinks immediately.

"Making bread?"

"Uh-huh," Ida says, easing the dough from the bowl onto the work surface. "I make a loaf every couple of days. Never buy one. Sometimes I make them for others, if there's a demand."

"I've never seen it made before," Harper admits.

Ida looks at her, eyebrows up in peaks. "You're kidding."

"No," Harper laughs. "Is that strange?"

"Round these parts, maybe," Ida says. She starts to work the dough.

"So, I'm curious as to what prompted this visit, Jane. Have there been more developments?" She folds the dough over, presses down hard with the ball of her hand, stretches it out, folds it over again. "Please tell me there isn't another young woman's been found."

"No, nothing like that. I just came to see you. I felt like I should, after what happened up at Wisher's Pond. I felt bad."

"For what?"

"For putting you through that, when there wasn't any real need. I just thought—"

"I'm glad you did take me there," Ida tells her, working the dough, her voice tight with effort. "It showed me you believed in me, that you don't think I'm nuts. Like they did back when they locked me up."

Harper stands and leans against the counter, watching Ida work. "I hoped you might pick up on something. A trace of something. It was a long shot, but at this point, I'll take any break I can get."

"Let me ask you something. How come you've worked your way to me after all these years? And what about the other families? He must have killed in the past thirty years. He must've."

Oh God, she is sharp.

"I'm going to be completely honest here, Ida. I need you to listen to what I have to tell you."

"Go on."

Harper starts at the beginning, and tells her the whole story. Ida listens while she works the dough, lets it rise a second time, and shapes it to go in the loaf pan.

"You haven't said a lot," Harper says. It's immeasurably hot, the air still and smothering.

They're out on the porch, listening to another of Ida's records, the smell of freshly baked bread wafting from within. "I don't know what to say. I guess I'm sad. No, angry, that those families have been lied to, that this man has been allowed to get away with killing young women all these years, with no one to stop him."

"I know how you feel, and I completely sympathize. They justified it as protecting the town."

Ida shakes her head in disgust. "Apple's rotten, no matter how much you polish it on your sleeve."

"Well, the truth is out now. And when we catch this guy, the whole world will know it, I promise," Harper says. "But that's why we can't contact the other families. They don't know their daughters died in such a way."

"So all you have is me, huh?"

"Pretty much," Harper sighs.

Ida looks out at the horizon, where it gets hazy, her eyes narrowed. "Four years they locked me up at the mental hospital, thinkin' I was nuts. Four years. I wasn't allowed music, despite asking for some over and over again. I was a prisoner. They didn't let me out of my room at night, not after I tried to kill myself. All I've ever wanted is to heal. That's why I live out here, Jane. I need space to fix myself, sort my head out. But more than that, I guess I've wanted to feel understood."

"Ida—" Harper starts to speak, but her phone buzzes in her pocket. She pulls it out, looks down at the screen.

```
Dead  end  on  Ruby's  work  friends.  No
record  of  who  was  employed  there.  How's
it  going?  Where  are  you?—SR
```

She types back quickly:

```
Still  at  Ida's.  I've  told  her  everything.
Will  explain  later.
```

His response is immediate.

```
Ok.  Take  care  of  yourself.  Talk  to  you
later.—SR
```

Harper is about to put it away when it vibrates again.

```
BTW,  last  night  was  amazing.  We  need
to  discuss  at  some  point.  I  think  I've
fallen  for  you,  Jane.  I  hope  you  feel
the  same.  Sorry  to  put  this  on  you,  but
I  need  to  say  it.—SR
```

"Trouble?" Ida asks quietly, watching her put the phone away.

"No," Harper says.

Did Stu just say he loves me? Is that what that text was?

"You don't know what it means to me that you believe what I'm sayin'," Ida tells Harper. "I've waited so long."

"Don't mention it."

Ida gets up. "You want to stay for dinner? I'm doing a chicken. And I've got beers in the fridge, nice and cold."

Harper smiles up at her. "You had me at beers. And I *am* kind of suspended, after all."

Ida heads back inside. "Be right back."

Harper thinks for a moment, takes her phone back out, and types a reply to Stu's last text:

```
I can't think about us until this case
is over. That's not me saying no to us.
That's me saying let's wait. I hope you
understand. X
```

"Here you go." Ida hands her a cold beer.

"Cheers." Harper clinks her bottle against Ida's and takes a long, hearty swallow. "Ah, that's good."

"So, how goes the investigation in general? Are you any closer to catching him?" Ida asks her.

Harper shakes her head. "No. We have DNA, but nothing to match it to. We have a description of his car, but that's a dead end. Everything we've tried has come to nothing."

"Because the truth has been buried so long," Ida offers.

"That, and the cases weren't investigated properly back in the day. Any details that might have helped us aren't there any longer."

Ida swallows some beer. "I remember there was a very nice detective working the case in the beginning. He came to my mother's funeral."

"I know him. We spoke to him. He directed me to you," Harper tells her. "I actually intended on calling him. He might be able to tell me something else."

She finds the number for the retirement home on her phone. She calls it, holding the phone to her ear. "Hello . . . Yes, I know it's a long shot . . . I'm a detective with the Hope's Peak PD . . . Yes, that's the one . . . uh-huh . . . The patient is Lloyd Claymore . . . Yes, I can wait . . ." She looks at Ida, feels her heart sink as she listens to the person on the other end. "Oh. No, no, no, I understand . . . Yes I will . . . Thank you for your help."

"Jane?"

Harper puts her phone away. "He's gone. Passed away two nights ago."

Ida clamps a hand to her mouth. "My God. Natural causes?"

"Yes."

"That's so sad. He was a lovely man," Ida says. "Tried his best to get to the bottom of my mother's murder."

All that Harper can think is, *He'll never answer for the crimes he covered up. And I'll never truly know if he regrets it.*

Ida hoists the beer in front of her. "To Detective Lloyd Claymore."

And unsolved cases, Harper thinks.

11

The chicken was roasted with lemon and sprigs of thyme from Ida's herb garden. She sautéed potatoes and served them with steamed greens. *Of course*, Ida let a giant knob of butter melt over the greens, and *of course*, the pair of them had one too many beers to wash it all down.

Now Jane Harper is asleep on Ida's sofa, snoring steadily. There came a point when Ida knew Jane would end up staying the night—there was no way she could've driven home safely. Ida fetches a thick blanket, knowing how cold the house gets at night sometimes, even when the days are so hot. She covers Harper over and turns off the TV, but puts a small lamp on in its place—that way the detective will remember where she is, instead of waking in the dark in a strange house. As she begins to leave, Ida rests her palm on Harper's head.

"There you are, sugar. You rest easy now."

The lamp flickers and the room warms slightly.

The white mist rises, the connection is made, and Ida sees something take shape in her mind's eye, a memory, a dream, something from Harper's subconscious: *removing her wedding ring and setting it down on a dresser. Looking around a house as if she'll never see it again. Licking the edge of an envelope before sealing the letter inside. Setting the envelope next to the abandoned wedding ring.*

And then: *Harper driving away from the house, belongings in boxes in her car. Looking back in the mirror and not feeling deflated, or sad, but liberated. Leaving, walking away from hard situations comes easily. It's a comfort to her, not being rooted in any one spot.*

Ida removes her hand, breaking the tenuous connection.

"But rooted is what you want, ain't it, sugar?"

She thinks of Bob Dylan singing "Like A Rolling Stone." That's Harper, a stone without a home, rolling from place to place. On her own.

Ida goes to bed, leaving Harper to dream her dreams in private, hoping that with enough rest her visitor might find some peace. But for Ida there will be none. That night, sleep finds her.

And, in her dreams, so does *he*.

"Oh thank Christ you're here, Lester!" Ceeli lets him in, closing the door behind them. She leads him into the living room and they sit on the sofa. There are a few lights on in the house, and darkness beyond the windows. "I've been worried sick. I didn't know what was happening."

She can see Lester's shock at her appearance. Her eyes have nearly closed up, the bruising has come out fully. She is talking funny because her jaw doesn't want to work.

"What'd he do to you?" he asks her.

"Beat me. I thought he was gonna kill me when he found out about us," she says. "What happened when he got to your house? You haven't been answering your phone."

"Difconnected it."

"Oh." Ceeli studies his face. "So . . . what happened?"

Lester licks his top lip, the one that's twisted up in the center, revealing his teeth and gums. "Nothin'. He didn't fhow."

She frowns. "He didn't? That's strange."

Lester shrugs.

"Maybe he went off someplace," Ceeli says, though her tone does little to hide the fact she is unconvinced.

Lester scratches the side of his face. "How'd he find out?"

"Julie next door, she told him. I think maybe she caught us up to something," Ceeli tells him. She reaches out, takes his hand in hers, gives it a squeeze. "But don't worry, honey. It's out in the open now. We can be together. And there ain't gonna be no worryin' about Mack, Julie, or anyone else."

Lester pulls his hand away. "Don't want that."

"Lester honey?"

He puts his hands on her shoulders, forces her back on the sofa till she's lying in front of him. She looks nervous, a little scared. And he can see it—she's excited. "Thif if what I want," he says.

"Oh, honey, I wish I could . . . I'm so sore."

Lester lies on top of her. He kisses the side of her neck, his warped lips making sucking noises on her skin.

"Please . . . ," Ceeli begs him.

He looks at her blackened, puffy face. Her sad eyes peering out from deep bruises.

"You want to know how it feelf?"

Ceeli struggles, but he is strong. He is experienced. She lets out the beginnings of a scream as he tears her clothes off and clamps his hand over her mouth. She tries to hit him with her right arm. Lester pins the arm up over her head, holding it against the armrest of the sofa.

He looks into her eyes. "You're trouble. You're *all* trouble. But *they* are different. They're good. You . . . you're *nothing*."

Lester's grip eases, and for the briefest second, Ceeli thinks he is letting her go, but then he brings a cushion down on her face. Pressing, pressing, pressing . . .

All those times he managed to restrain himself from killing her, from strangling her to death. Now he can follow it through. Lester lifts the cushion, throws it to one side, and grips her neck in his bare hands. Ceeli tries to pull his forearms away, but his arms are locked. She tries to fight, tries to breathe, suck in one last breath. Lester shifts his grip so he can manage it with one hand, and yanks down his bottoms to grant freedom to his throbbing cock. Ceeli passes out in front of him. Lester lets go, reaches into his pants, and removes the white mask, the belt. He puts it on and there's a change in the air. He has arrived.

Lester slaps Ceeli around the face. Her eyes open, then widen at the sight of him with the mask on.

Now you'll feel it.

Julie turns off all the lights and carries her book upstairs. She's been a fan of Stephen King for years, but his latest fails to keep her attention. And yet sometimes books have a way of surprising you. You read fifty pages, thinking it isn't connecting, and then something clicks and you're in. She thinks she'll give Mr. King another night or so of reading, to give him the benefit of the doubt, but it's not looking hopeful.

Julie puts the book down and heads to the bathroom. She turns on the water, squeezes toothpaste on her electric toothbrush, and puts it in her mouth. It vibrates away as she works it around her mouth, massaging her gums, getting in all the nooks and crannies.

SMASH!

Julie stops the toothbrush and listens. All is silent. She puts the brush back in her mouth, turns it on, dismissing the sound. Maybe she's hearing things. Maybe it's something outside.

SMASH!

She stands there, looking in the mirror, as if her reflection can explain to her the noise coming from downstairs. She stops the toothbrush, spits into the sink, and steps out on the landing. The bottom of the house is dark. Still. Quiet.

Julie watches the stairs for movement, but there is none.

Call the police.

She doesn't know what to do. What if it's a cat that got in? That happened once before—she locked up for the night and didn't realize a cat had gotten into the house during the afternoon. In the middle of the night, she woke to find it bouncing off the walls, smashing all of her china.

Julie throws the light on in the hall and starts down the stairs.

What if it's not?

She hesitates, the step under her foot creaking with her weight. That's when she sees him. He has a white hood on his head, belt tight around his neck. He looks up at her with dark eyes.

Julie backs up, blood turned to ice water. The man takes one step at a time. She can hear his breathing. She can feel his eyes burning into her. She backs up against something hard. It's the wall next to the bathroom door.

Quick!

She darts inside the bathroom and slams the door, fumbling with the latch, trying to get it to move with fingers that are numb, hands that have turned to jelly. An incredible weight shoves the door toward her, smashing her in the face. Julie falls back, and the door thunders against the tiles on the wall. The man stands in the doorway. She whimpers, looking up at him, her heart jackhammering under her nightshirt. Tears fill her eyes as he walks toward her, as he dominates her vision.

"What are you going to do to me?" she whispers, her throat so dry she can barely form words.

The man bends down, face inches from hers. "What d'you think?"

◆ ◆ ◆

He finishes and gets up. Carefully, he unbuckles the belt around his neck, then handles the delicate white material of the torn hood, almost as though he were cradling a newborn. She's the first of his victims to get anywhere near it. He can't believe she's ripped it. Lester folds the hood, slips it into his pocket. On his way out of the bathroom, he flips the switch and the light goes off.

"Night," he says as he goes down the stairs and out through the back door. Glass lies in shattered pieces on the floor. It crunches underfoot as he flees into the night.

No one saw him arrive. No one sees him leave. He is a ghost among the living. The giver of freedom.

The taker of life.

12

Someone is humming.

Harper opens her eyes and feels a sharp stabbing pain in the middle of her forehead. She sits up, groggy, feeling the worse for wear. "Christ, what happened to me?"

Ida walks in, apron on, smile on her face. "Morning."

"Morning," Harper croaks. She looks at the happy black woman standing in front of her, wondering how she could possibly be tip-top while she feels like death personified. "You're not hung over?"

"No! You want coffee?"

"Yes, please God," Harper says, getting up gingerly, as if she's a patient who's been operated on. "Do you mind if I use your bathroom?"

"Not at all. You know where you're going. Have a shower, if you like. I left you out some towels. I had an inkling you might have a change of clothes in your car, and found all that in your trunk. Sorry, I had to use your keys. I didn't touch any of your stuff."

"Wow, you're really thorough," Harper says, thinking of the overnight bag she always takes with her. There's everything in there—change of clothes, toothbrush, toothpaste, perfume, hairbrush . . . even condoms, should she need them.

Hope she didn't poke around in there . . .

"Go on up, Jane. Coffee will be waiting for you."

"Thanks," Harper says, pausing on the steps. "Hey, you're a really nice person, Ida. Does anyone ever tell you that?"

"I don't think so."

"Well, they should," Harper says. A half hour later she is in fresh clothes, hair still damp from the shower, and she feels better. It makes all the difference in the world just brushing her teeth. One of the things that's always made her laugh is when, in a movie, two lovers wake up after having a drunken one-night stand, and full-on kiss. She could never do that.

Last thing I want is to exchange death breath.

"Have a seat, sugar," Ida says. "Bet that feels better, don't it?"

"Oh yeah," Harper says, smiling. She looks at the clock on the wall. "Jesus, is that really the time?"

Ida puts a mug of coffee in front of her. "Thought I'd let you sleep. You looked tired last night."

"I was," Harper agrees. "I needed some rest, I think."

Stu calls. Harper takes it outside. "Hey," she says, holding the phone to her ear.

"You alright? I didn't hear from you last night."

"I stayed here at Ida's."

A second of silence, then: "Isn't that, like, a bit weird?"

"No, I don't think so. It feels like I've known her for ages."

"I know, Jane, but—"

"Stu, honestly, I'm fine. How about you?"

"Albie called me. There's a murder scene bears a close resemblance to Magnolia, Alma, and Gertie. Raped and strangled. It's in a house.

He's at the scene now. They pulled DNA and are comparing it to what we have on file so far. Albie said he won't say dick about this to Morelli, before you start worryin'."

"Wow. Okay. I didn't expect that," Harper says. "I'll get there as soon as I can."

"Look, let me check it out; I'll let you know what I find. There's nothing you can do right now. I promise I'll call soon as I can, and let you know what's going on."

"Okay," Harper says through gritted teeth. "But right away, you hear?"

"Yes, *mon capitaine*," Stu says. "And, uh, thanks for the reply last night. I didn't know what you'd make of my text. I actually thought it might be a mistake sending it."

"Why would you think that?"

"You're a hard girl to read, Jane. What with what happened at the station, and the way you took off the other night, I thought maybe you were having second thoughts."

"I took off because I wanted to be in my own bed," Harper tells him. "But that doesn't mean I *wanted* to leave yours."

A pause. "You realize that statement makes no sense, right?"

"Oh shut up. I'll talk to you later when you're not being so obtuse."

Stu laughs on the other end. "Okay," he says. "I love you, kiddo. I want you to know that."

"Stu, I . . ." Harper swallows. Her throat is dry. "Take care."

"I will."

The line goes dead and she puts the phone in her pocket. In that moment, on Ida's porch, with the sun high above the tree line, she feels a sudden pang of loneliness.

I don't know how she can live out here, Harper thinks. *It's peaceful, but there's such a thing as being* too *peaceful. I'm well rested having come here, but it's too far removed from everything.*

She feels as though she is at the bow of an ocean liner, leaning on the railings, gazing upon an endless vista of blue sky and even bluer sea. A sense of being lost in place and time.

But there is Stu, and there are the victims awaiting their retribution. And there is Ida, who is as much a victim herself as her mother was. They are the anchors keeping Harper tethered.

It's midday, and Ida has started her music. Robert Cray spills from inside the house—his clear tenor and riotous band causing the very air to quake.

I need to leave soon, Harper thinks. She sighs and goes in.

"Run this by me again?" Stu asks, looking at the broken glass on the floor.

"Yeah," Albie Goode says. He consults his notebook. "Victim's name is Julie Halbrook. Her sister was due to stop by, got no answer, came around the back, saw the broken glass, and called it in."

They walk to the hall. There are men and women working the carpet on the stairs, pulling glass fragments from the wiry fibers.

"And the body?" Stu asks, looking up to where the bathroom door is open.

"Officer attending the scene discovered her up there. She's been moved to the morgue."

"Right."

Albie flips through the pages. "Uh . . . found on her knees, raped. Strangled from behind, we think. Looked like she took a good beating, too."

Stu shakes his head. "Fuck."

A young police officer calls Albie over to her. "Excuse me a moment, Stu," Albie says.

"Sure, no problem."

Stu walks outside, stretches the stiff muscles in his back. Several neighbors have gathered on the other side of the street and are talking among themselves.

He dials Harper's number. "Hey."

"How're you doing?"

"They've already moved the body. Doesn't matter. It's the same MO, Jane. Aside from the fact she's white, and there was no crown. But it's too much of a coincidence for it to be anything else."

"God."

"I know," Stu says with a sigh. "Thought I'd give you the update. We should have access to their reports in a couple of hours. We'll see how they do with any foreign DNA they find on the body."

"Yeah, we know how *that's* going to go, don't we?"

"Talk soon," Stu says, closing the phone.

The neighbors to the left of Julie Halbrook are being questioned by officers on their front lawn. Stu looks to the right—that house is dark and quiet.

He ducks under the yellow tape and crosses the lawn. The doorbell doesn't work so he knocks on the door, hard. When no response comes, he knocks again.

"We already tried that," a young police officer calls across. "No one home."

"Yeah, well . . ." Stu looks down the side of the house. It's overgrown and trashy, but there's a definite path there, stamped into the short grass. "Anyone tried the back?"

The officer shakes his head. "Want me to tag along?"

"Might be a good move."

He heads down the side of the house, right hand behind him, over his holster. He notices a window into the kitchen. He glances in, sees no movement, then makes his way around the back.

The door is open.

Stu pulls out his gun, holds it at the ready. "Pull your sidearm, officer."

The younger man swallows with nerves and fumbles his gun from the holster.

"Shouldn't we call some of the others over?"

Stu steps inside the threshold and calls out. "Hello?"

Nothing moves in the house. Stu signals for the officer to follow behind, and pushes on into the house, checking every room as he goes. Dining room. Living room. Pantry.

"Stick around down here. I'll clear the top," Stu whispers, already heading up the staircase before the officer can object in any way.

"Police department. Anybody home?" The steps creak with every footfall, but he continues up at his own pace. There is a stretch of bare wall at the very top, then a bathroom. Next to that, a bedroom. The door is ajar. Stu nudges it wide open with his foot and goes in with his gun ahead of him, checking every corner. He backs up, walks along the landing. The second bedroom is open; there's no one in there. "Clear!"

The officer is waiting for him at the bottom of the stairs. "What do you think happened here, Detective?"

Stu heads down the stairs, smiling. "Looks like they forgot to lock their back door, that's what."

Harper answers her phone: "Albie?"

Ida turns the music down while Harper is conversing.

"Hey, Harper."

"Stu told me you called him about a crime scene this morning."

"He did?"

"Yeah. I appreciate you keeping us in the loop."

"Don't mention it."

"So, did they find anything on the DNA?"

"Yes. DNA from the semen was a match, Harper."

Harper is shaking her head. "I don't know what this guy is doing, Albie. I don't understand him. His behavior is . . . erratic. Why now? Why go on a killing spree all of a sudden?"

"Beats me. It doesn't make any sense to me either."

Harper sighs. "Anything else?"

"The captain's pulling his hair out. What's left of it anyway. Member of the press tried to get in here."

"Jesus," Harper says. "We'll catch a break. Mark my words."

"Right you are, boss," Albie says, ending the call.

Ida lights a cigarette. "The woman that Detective Raley got called to . . . it's the same killer isn't it?"

"Looks that way, yes," Harper tells her. "DNA is a match."

Ida's hand goes to her neck. She watches as Harper rounds up her things, shoving them hastily into her bag. "How about meeting us in the parking lot next to the Buy N Save later?"

Ida sucks on the cigarette, blowing a steady trail of blue smoke out one side of her mouth. "Sure, no problem."

"You can always say no . . ."

She shakes her head. "No need to. We're in this together, am I right, sugar?"

Harper nods at the door. "I guess we are. I'll be in touch, Ida. Thanks for letting me stay."

"Don't you mention it. Now go, get gone," Ida says, waving her off.

13

Barnie looks at the three people standing in front of him, less than impressed.

"What's up?" Stu asks him. "Same arrangement as always, right?"

"Aaah, I'm afraid the stakes have gone up, Detective," Barnie says, drawing a sharp breath as he says it. "I'm risking my job letting you in with a civilian. Maybe I need a donation to my retirement fund."

Stu regards him incredulously, as if seeing him for the first time. "Are you fucking kidding me, Barnie?"

"Nope," he says, shaking his head. "I've had reporters trying to get in here. For all I know, they could be a test from management. See if I'm dirty. I don't want the extra risk without, you know, extra compensation, man."

"Yeah? That so?" Stu asks, walking around Barnie's desk to the other side.

Harper watches the exchange with growing alarm. "Stu, what're you doing?"

"Arresting this son of a bitch for attempting to extort a police officer," Stu says, pulling out his cuffs. Barnie tries to dodge him, but Barnie's too big.

"Hey! What the hell, Detective?" he cries as Stu slaps the cuffs on him, holding his arms behind his back. "Damn, that hurts."

"Sit down," Stu snarls at him. "We'll be quick, and if you keep your mouth shut, I won't mention this to your boss."

"Come on," Harper says, looking back at the front door. "Make sure they're locked."

Stu checks the control panel. "Yeah, they are."

Ida walks ahead of them—she knows the room. Her stomach pulls tight into a knot when she gets to the door, knowing what's behind it, picking up on the atmosphere of the place, the emptiness of it. They go inside, and Harper checks the board on the wall to find out who is where. Stu pulls Julie's body out, unfolding the sheet away from her face as if revealing an ancient artifact. Skin, milky white, looking like a snow queen lying there, her lips a startling shade of electric blue.

Harper's hand falls to Ida's shoulder. "Are you ready?"

Ida swallows. "Yes. But bring that chair over, so I can sit when I'm done. Save me from hitting the floor like a bag of feed."

"Got it," Stu says, fetching the office chair from the other side of the room.

Ida places her hand on the woman's forehead and sinks into the woman, sinks into her skin.

That telltale warmth fills the room and the low lights dim further.

That voice. There's something about that voice. Julie tries to scramble to the side, but the man is quick. He steps in her way, a little chuckle coming from beneath the mask. Julie lashes out as he grapples to control her, dropping to his knees, and she somehow snags his head covering. Julie pulls and it rips, separating from the section pinned by the belt.

She knows him. His ugly, brutish face is red-hot and flustered from battling her on the bathroom floor. She is about to say his name when his right arm goes back, and Julie knows what is coming. His fist hits her and it's like a million-watt bulb explodes in her brain.

Her vision swims. The mask hangs from the belt around his neck, and he glares at her.

"That wafn't nife."

"Listen . . . what are you doing?" Julie murmurs, half dazed from the blow.

He grabs her hair and forces her to turn around. "On your kneef."

"No!" Julie struggles, but his iron grip on her hair stops her. He's not letting go.

A part of her speaks up: Let him do what he's going to do. You might live. Cooperate and you might live.

Sobbing, Julie has her back to him, and she lowers herself forward, exposing her rear end to him. She hears him deal with his jeans. His breathing comes hurried, almost snorting with excitement. The pain of him forcing his way inside makes her cry out, makes her try to fight him off again. He shifts around behind her, pulls her head back by her hair. Julie screams.

He holds her hair with his right hand, and reaches around with his left. He finds the soft, delicate flesh of her bare throat and caresses it with his fingers, all the while forcing himself into her.

"You gotta know when to keep your mouth fhut."

His left hand closes on her throat and he grits his teeth, growling like an animal as he crushes Julie's windpipe. Taking the spark of life and crushing it in his hands.

Shutting out the light.

Ida flops back, the connection broken, and her backside finds the chair. She sags into it, exhausted. Stu hurriedly pushes the body back into cold storage and closes the door. Harper squats next to Ida. "Are you okay?"

She has one hand to her head, as if it threatens to blow apart. "Yes . . . yes, I'll be fine . . . Just give me a minute . . ."

"What did you see?" Stu asks her.

Ida swallows. "You know what he did. Beat her. Raped her from behind. Strangled the life out of her. But she knew him. She tore his mask off."

"You saw his face?"

Ida frowns, remembering. "Vaguely. It was a blur. But I know one thing. He has some kind of problem with his mouth. He speaks with a li*sp*. He's got some kind of facial deformity."

"This is great, Ida. Any name?"

She shakes her head. "Sorry."

"No, no, no." Harper holds Ida's hand. "You did great."

"I don't think we'll be able to do this again," Stu says.

"Not with Fat Ass at the counter, we won't." Harper checks outside the door. There's no one else there. "Ida, can you stand, do you think?"

"I can try."

Harper waves Stu over. "Get her other side. We'll walk her out."

They position her arms around their shoulders and steer her into the hall. When they get near the desk, Stu sets about freeing Barnie from his handcuffs while Harper continues with Ida toward the car.

Barnie rubs his wrists. "What's to stop me from reporting you for this?"

"Nothing," Stu admits. "But just remember, I know where you live, Barnie. It wouldn't be a very good move."

The fat man looks down at the floor.

Stu taps the side of Barnie's flabby face. "Lesson learned. Don't get greedy."

"Ida, let me drop you at my place. You can rest there. I don't want you driving home in the dark the way you are," Harper says, looking at her in the backseat. She looks worse than she did the first time around, after doing a reading of Gertie Wilson's body. Drained.

Ida shakes her head. "No . . . I'll be fine to drive. Honestly."

"No offense, but you look like death," Stu tells her as Harper starts the engine.

"Trust me, sugar, I feel like it," Ida concedes.

"Then it's settled. I'll drop you at my apartment; then I want to head to the station," Harper says.

"Really? You know what time it is?" Stu asks. "It's late!"

"Yeah, well, doesn't matter. We need to search the records, Stu. And we can't do that in the daylight because we're not supposed to be there."

Stu shrugs. "Point made."

"What about my truck?" Ida asks.

"Stu can drive it back. His car's parked at my place."

"Okay," Ida says.

Stu hisses: "Thanks for volunteering me."

"Anytime," Harper says with a smile.

Harper ushers Ida into her bed, pulling the covers up over her.

"Do you want a light on?" she asks her, but Ida is already asleep. She closes the bedroom door and goes to the kitchen, where Stu is hunting in the fridge for a drink.

"You don't have a Coke in here?"

Harper shakes her head. "I don't buy them."

"You don't? What do you drink?"

She shrugs. "I don't know . . . water?"

Stu pulls a bottle from the fridge. "Too early for Chardonnay."

"Come on. Let's get going. I'll buy you a coffee later," Harper tells him, holding the front door to her apartment open for him.

"You say it like that, but it's really because you want to buy a coffee for yourself, isn't it?"

"Well I don't want to leave you out," she tells him.

There is minimal staff on duty, and no one takes any notice when Harper and Stu walk into the station, heading straight for the basement. Down there, they use the computer access terminal in the corner—better to do it out of sight than at one of their desks, where they might draw attention. It allows them to gain access to the same generic files as anyone with limited clearance throughout the entire building.

Harper hovers over Stu's shoulder as he pulls up hospital records for the immediate and surrounding area.

"So how old do we think this guy is?"

"When he killed Ruby in nineteen eighty-five, he probably was in his twenties or thirties at least. Ruby was twenty-four years old when he murdered her," Harper says.

Stu does the math, sounding it out so that Harper can chime in if needed. "If he was twenty back then, that'd make him fifty now. Even saying he was forty, he'd be seventy now. I think at the extreme end of the scale, he'll be eighty—although the fact he'd need strength and a certain physicality to carry out these murders rules out the possibility of him being that old, I guess. So, fifty years old in nineteen eighty-five, which means he would have been born nineteen thirty-five."

"Make the search range from thirty-five onwards to, like, the late sixties. Let's see what we come up with," Harper tells him.

Stu taps the search range in, selects the criteria, and lets it run.

"Ah, seven names," he says, leaning toward the screen. "All born with facial irregularities between nineteen thirty-five and nineteen sixty-nine."

"Send it to the printer," Harper tells him, walking back and forth. "I feel like we're finally closing in now."

Stu finds the hospital record for each name and does a quick check. "Three of these are deceased. That leaves us four. I'm printing their addresses and physical attributes now."

"Great. But I think it's a bit late now to go knocking on doors."

"Yeah I'm with you. We'll hit it first thing tomorrow," Stu says. "Not that I'm not eager to find this bastard."

"We're really close now." Harper takes his face in both hands. "I'm so thrilled I could kiss you."

"Why don't you?"

She leans down, presses her lips hard against his. Stu gets to his feet and grabs her around the waist, picking her up. He walks with her in his arms, her legs hooked around his waist, the two kissing passionately. When Stu's knees hit one of the research desks, he lowers Harper to it. The printer spews out paper in the corner as he wrestles Harper's pants down to her ankles, then off, and drops them on the floor. Harper yanks his belt from the buckle and unbuttons his fly.

There is nothing to say, just the urgent need, the sudden slapping of skin on skin, the two of them grunting, carnal and primitive. It's over in less than a minute, Stu holding her legs together, her feet pinned by the side of his face. Harper panting from the sudden rush of her orgasm, the risk of getting caught only heightening the experience.

Catching his breath, Stu looks at her.

Harper reaches down, slaps his behind. "I think the printer's stopped."

The body the body the body.

Lester goes to the car and pops the trunk. The smell that rises from Ceeli's body is overwhelming, but nothing he hasn't dealt with before. He reaches in, lifts her onto his shoulders, and carries her. She has baked in the trunk of the car, and her body is swollen, but she's still light.

He carries her through the backyard, to the shed. The door is open and he's set a chair in there. Grunting, he stoops down and deposits her in it. Ceeli immediately flops to one side, but with a bit of maneuvering, he gets her sitting in it just right.

As she died, he took her, clamping the cushion down on her face so hard she was unable to take a breath. He built to his climax, grunting with the effort, and Ceeli suddenly relaxed around him. That was how he knew she was gone. Her hands stopped fighting him, stopped scratching at his arms. Her legs fell slack on either side of his hips.

Remembering the sensation makes him groan, makes him ache all over, fills his head with brain sparkle.

Lester admires her, sitting there with her chin resting on her chest, her ashy color, her swelling, the stink rising from her dead body. And the horror frozen on her face.

"There you are," he says, grinning, already feeling the stiffening in his pants at the prospect of having her there with him. "You're home."

He doesn't know why he didn't get started before, but then it was never his plan to take Ceeli for his own. It just happened naturally, like a dribble of water breaking away from the main stream to become a tributary of its own. Lester walks around the side of the house, and down through the long grass that borders the house and the woods. He feels the supplejack with his fingers, determining whether they're what's needed. He selects the best, the process a calming one. Lester gathers them together and thinks, *These will make an excellent crown for Ceeli. Something Mack should have done for her. Now I'm here to make her my princess.*

Harper parks her car in front of her house. She and Stu get out, and Harper glances at his car, parked across the street. "I'd invite you in, but . . ."

"I know," Stu says. "Another time."

"Definitely," Harper says.

They kiss, Stu holding her by the waist. "We take two names each, yeah?"

"Uh-huh. You're sure we shouldn't involve the rest of the department in this?" Harper asks him. "At least Captain Morelli. Surely we should get in touch with him, let him know what's happened."

"Not yet. Let's be sure, first. Smoke him out, Jane. Make him blow his own cover."

"Damn, Stu. You're talking like a real detective!"

Stu crosses the street, turns back to look at her. "See you tomorrow."

Harper waves him off, then goes inside. The apartment is how she left it. She checks on Ida, who is lying in the fetal position in her bed. She pours herself two fingers of scotch and sits on the sofa. She doesn't even touch the drink before she's asleep.

14

It's approaching midday when Stu leaves the home of the first name on his list. David Jenson. Born with a severe cleft lip that was corrected when he was eight, leaving a scar, but very little warping of his facial features. He phones Harper.

"One down, one to go."

"How did you make out?"

"He's about the right age, but there's no way he's the killer. He had a stroke and lost all strength in his arms, besides the fact that his sister can vouch for his whereabouts. To rape and kill a young woman, it takes a fair bit of strength."

"You're beginning to sound experienced in this area, Stu."

"I am, pretty much. Not that I'd like to be," he says, climbing into his car and firing up the engine. "I'm gonna go visit Lester Simmons, see what I turn up. This one will probably be missing his arms and legs, dragging his ass around all day on a goddamned skateboard."

"Be careful, partner."

"I will."

"As it turns out, I've got my last one, too. I'm convinced—one of these names must be the killer."

"Well, looks like we'll find out real soon."

"I'll let you know, soon as I'm done here," Harper tells him.

"Roger, roger."

Harper parks the car. "Ida, why don't you wait here, okay?"

"You don't need me?" Ida asks her.

"I don't think so. I have a good nose for this stuff. Besides, I'll be able to tell from what he has to say," Harper explains. "I'll be fine."

"Mind if I listen to the stereo?"

Harper laughs. "Of course not."

It's hot out. Harper wears a light-blue shirt, rolled up at the sleeves, as open at the chest as she dares—though she wears a thin vest beneath. She has a notebook in one arm, a file. Her gun bulges in its holster at her right hip.

The house is pleasant enough, nestled among a row of similar houses, a well-kept lawn in the front. The whole street is nice, she concludes, though sometimes it's the brightest houses that hide the darkest interiors.

Harper rings the doorbell and waits. She is about to ring it again when a woman in her fifties, hair going to gray, answers the door. "Yes?"

"Hello, I'm Detective Jane Harper. I'd like to speak to George Armistad? Is he home?"

The woman swallows. "I'm afraid not."

"Is he out? Any idea how long he'll be, or when he'll be back?"

"No," the woman says, shaking her head. It's now that Harper notices the bags under her eyes, the pale complexion of her skin. Her short nails that look bitten rather than clipped. "I'm afraid George is no longer with us."

Harper feels the wind rush out of her. "What?" she says softly, voice barely a whisper.

Tears come to the woman. "He passed away in his sleep not two nights ago. I'm really very sorry, Detective."

"Right," Harper says, looking down at her notebook, just to be able to look away from the woman in her grief.

"I'm really not in the right frame for questions right now, Detective. So . . ."

She starts to close the door. Harper nods, steps back, and the door shuts. She turns and heads back to the car. There's a distinct difference between dealing with a dead body and the family of the dead. The survivors who have to bear the pain and anguish.

Back in the car, Ida has found a station playing "Wicked Game" and is sitting in the passenger seat, singing along to it. Harper gets behind the wheel, but before she starts the engine, the realization hits her—the man Stu is going to meet may very well be the killer.

"What're we doing now?" Ida asks.

Harper calls Stu on the hands-free. It goes straight to voice mail. She turns the key, handing Ida her cell. "Keep trying him, Ida."

Stu parks away from Lester Simmons's house. Much like Ida, he lives apart from the rest of town. His home lies down a dirt road, a couple of minutes' drive from suburbia. The houses out here are big and old and come with plenty of land. Stu leaves his car door open, and gets closer on foot, careful to stay out of sight. He can hear his phone ringing, and he knows who it will be and why. Harper will tell him this last name on the list is very likely their killer. She'll tell him to wait for her, to get backup. But suppose they're wrong—suppose he calls all that in, and the man is innocent. Or doesn't even live here. The hospital records can be only so accurate . . .

He returns to the car, grabs his phone, and switches it to silent but keeps the vibration on so that he can feel it ringing in his pocket. Stu locks the car, then pulls his sidearm out, checking the clip before sliding the gun back into the holster. He looks up at the house, and the sight of it sends a cold shiver down the back of his neck.

Well, here we go.

"Where does this guy live?" Ida asks.

"I don't know," Harper says. "Do me a favor, Ida. Open that file there. The printouts are in the back."

Ida pulls several loose pages out. "These?"

"That's it. You're looking for Lester Simmons," Harper tells her, checking her mirrors and changing lanes. "I know I'm headed in the right direction, but I need the actual address."

"Okay, sugar," Ida says. "Ah, it's here. Got it."

"D'you know how to use Google Maps?"

Ida just looks at her. "Google what?"

"Never mind. I'll have to pull over for a second."

More time wasted, she thinks. *I know what he'll be doing. He'll be knocking on the door, confronting the guy. He won't wait.*

She finds a place to stop and asks Ida for the phone. The map takes a moment to load, and now she knows where she's going. Still, she clips the phone back into its holder so that she can follow the map if she gets lost.

Her palms are sweaty on the steering wheel as she weaves through the traffic.

All she can think is, *He won't wait.*

Lester strokes Ceeli's hair. He is naked but for his head. The torn hood is on; the belt is pulled tight, held in place with the buckle.

He pulls Ceeli's head back and strokes his cock in her puffy face, rolling his eyes with the thrill of it, the tingle in every fiber of his being at performing such an act.

Lester pleasures himself, reveling in the moment, knowing it will come to an end. Ceeli will have to be moved. He'll have to burn her body the way he burned Mack's. But for now, it is glorious.

I feel like a new man.

He once watched a program on television that showed a pupa sealing itself in a cocoon, emerging some time later as a beautiful butterfly. A different beast altogether. After all these years, Lester knows it is his turn.

The man Mama wanted me to be.

Lester's grip tightens on Ceeli's hair, and his head jerks back, groaning, as wave after wave of euphoria washes over him . . .

Stu rings the doorbell and waits. When nothing happens he presses it again, tries to see through a dirty, dusty window if there is movement in the house.

None that he can see.

He takes out his gun and walks around the side. There's a gate there and he has to reach over the top to unlatch it. It squeaks on its rusted hinges, and Stu's hand flexes on the gun. The backyard is trashy, overgrown in places. There's a rusted swing. Old trash cans. Stu looks at the house. The door is open a shade, swinging back and forth on the frame as the breeze nudges it.

Someone's home.

There is a shed in the yard, but he dismisses it. Lester Simmons has to live here and, chances are, he's in the house.

He moves toward the door.

Lester hears the squeak of the gate and watches from one of the shed windows as a lawman stalks across his yard, heading straight for the house.

His mother's voice tickles like hairy spider legs inside his ear.

We don't have no truck with people invadin' our property lester baby you go get him you teach him a lesson he won't soon forget . . .

"Yes, Mama."

When the man's slipped inside the house, Lester bounds across the lawn and goes after him.

15

As she drives, Harper's head is foggy, awash with trepidation and a hundred different emotions.

"You alright, sugar?" Ida asks her. "You look ill."

"I'm okay," Harper lies. She feels sick to her stomach with worry. She wishes Stu were different, that he'd wait. But she knows he won't. It just feels right that the last name on that list is the name of the killer.

Ida looks at the phone on the dash. "Don't look like we've got much longer to go."

"Say, Ida, do you think things will change for you when this guy is caught?" Harper asks her, just to get her mind off what they're driving toward.

"Perhaps," Ida says mysteriously. "I think that maybe they might."

"Would you ever sell your house? Move closer to the town?"

Ida looks out the window, her face unreadable. "I don't know. That's a lot."

"I know it is."

When Harper thinks that Ida won't say anything more, she does. "I'll cross that bridge when I come to it."

He can hear the man walking farther into the house. Lester lifts the axe he keeps by the fridge and adjusts his grip on the worn handle. He creeps from the kitchen to the main entrance, where the man stands with his back to him. Lester's bare feet on the dusty floor make no sound; he holds his breath and is silent as a shadow.

The man is deciding whether to go to the other side of the house or straight upstairs. But he spends too long thinking it over. In the seconds he has hesitated, Lester has closed the gap.

A noise—Lester's foot scrapes the hard, cold floor as he raises the axe—makes the man turn around, gun coming up. Lester hacks down. The axe slices through the front of the man's chest. He staggers back, fires his gun to the side. Thunder fills the inside of the house, and Lester has to resist the urge to clamp his hands on his ears.

No. Finish the job.

He brings the axe down again, this time into the man's shoulder. The heavy blade hacks into him and gets wedged in his shoulder blade. The man lets loose a gargled scream that dies as he falls to the floor. Blood spews from where the axe juts up from his convulsing body.

Lester kicks the man's gun away. It skitters across the floor. He puts one boot against the man's chest, and tries to pull the axe free with both hands.

"That'*f*it," Lester says, grunting with effort. "Come to Papa."

Harper lowers her window, pulling up alongside Stu's car. "Damn . . ."

A bloodcurdling scream pierces the silence. Ida grabs Harper's hand and squeezes, hard.

"Oh no," she gasps, looking up at the house.

Harper throws her door open. She passes Ida her phone. "You know how to work a cell phone, right?"

"I can figure it out."

"Go into my contacts. Find Dudley. Call him. Tell him to get here. The address is on that piece of paper. Tell them everything that's gone down here."

"I will."

Another scream rises, then fades away to nothing. Harper can barely think. "Stay in the car. Press that button there to lock the doors from the inside," she tells her, walking away, pulling her gun from the holster.

"Jane!"

She turns back.

"Be careful."

Harper runs to the house.

The man is dying. Lester looks at him, the axe in his hands dripping dark-red blood.

"How doe*f* it feel?"

The man frowns, gasping for air, looking at him with a mixture of confusion and desperation. As Lester squats down next to him, the man looks away, a big tear running from his eye, rolling down his cheek. His breath catches; there is a long moment when nothing else happens, then a release of air, one final exhalation.

Lester stands up and considers the man in his hall. There is blood everywhere, mixed in with the dirt on the floor. Perhaps he should cut him into pieces the way he did with Mack . . . Wouldn't that make sense?

He hears the unmistakable sound of footsteps crunching their way toward the house. The front door is locked. Whoever is coming is likely looking for the man he's just killed. If they come in by the back door, they'll see him lying there in the hall. They might hesitate, back off, and call for help.

Lester wants them to come in. He wants to cut them into chunks and watch them die, watch them draw their last breath. Quickly, he runs to the front door and unlocks it so whoever it is can walk straight in.

Then, he hides.

She tries the handle. The front door is unlocked. Harper eases it open with her foot, weapon at the ready, and moves inside. It's dark compared to the brightness outside, and it takes a second for her eyes to adjust. There is a staircase, doors to the left and right. On the floor in front of her, a crumpled form lies in a widening pool of scarlet blood—Stu. Harper fights the impulse to run to his side. She watches every angle, carefully crossing the entrance hall and dropping to one knee beside him.

"Oh God . . ."

It's obvious he's gone, even before she puts her fingers to his neck and attempts to find a pulse. His clammy skin is already cool to the touch.

The tears come, but she fights them back, swallows them down inside for later. There is blood everywhere, his whole body is covered in it. Harper tries not to look at where he's been cut—or hacked—into. She reaches out and touches his face.

If I just look at his face, he could be sleeping.

Later, she will find a dark, quiet place. She will drink; she will cry; she will let everything out. But for now, her training kicks in. Harper knows that what she is going through, what she is feeling, must be bottled up inside.

There's a creak, a foot passing on a floorboard, and she is up, gun in front of her. There is a door to her left, leading to a series of shadowy rooms. A door to the right opens into a scruffy kitchen. The whole place is covered in dirt and stinks to high heaven.

Another creak of old wood. Fine dust filtering down from the ceiling.

Harper looks up at the big staircase, at the landing on either side of it over her head. She holds her gun at the ready and backs her way up to the bottom step, watching for signs of movement from the landing. It is empty. Her heart hammers in her chest, her blood pounding through her veins. She reaches the top step and has to decide: left or right.

Should I call out? Get him to surrender?

Harper dismisses the idea right away. Her hands flex on the gun. Her palms are sweaty. She goes to the left, back to the wall. The door on the other side is shut. She might've heard it close behind him if he'd gone that way. That leaves the door she is edging toward, swallowing spit to lubricate the sore dryness of her throat, sweat pouring down her back. She glances down, to the bottom of the stairs, where Stu's body rests in a bloodbath.

"Stay put, we're on our way," Dudley tells Ida on the phone.

"Jane told me to call . . ."

"Listen to me. Lock the doors, roll up the windows," Dudley says. "Stay where you are. Backup is coming."

Ida ends the call and is left with the phone, the silence of the car, the house in front of her. She unlocks the door and gets out, gripping the cell phone tight in her hand. A thought comes to her. A name. It howls in her head like a storm wind rushing under the eaves: *Jane.*

Harper licks her lips, swallows, gets ready to peer around the edge of the door frame. There's no way he's on the other side of the landing . . . but what if he is? What if he got the door shut so quietly she didn't hear it? Now she's not so sure.

I need to call him out.

Everything inside her begs her not to do it.

"This is Jane Harper! Hope's Peak PD!" she yells at the top of her lungs, waiting for something to happen, waiting for a sound, for anything to indicate the killer has heard her.

Nothing.

Harper clears her throat. Sweat trickles down one side of her face. She cocks her head, wipes it away on her shoulder. The air in the house doesn't move; it is hot and stuffy. Funky with mildew, dirt, and grime.

Decay.

A floorboard creaks, ever so slightly, on the other side of the wall she is standing against.

He's there. He's listening. If he doesn't come out you're gonna have to swing around the door frame and take a shot.

She turns, trying to follow the sound with her gun. The wall behind her bursts apart, explodes, throwing her forward against the railing. A cloud of plaster, dust, and debris flies around her. Harper barely registers the way the hard railing jams into her midsection before a body crashes into her. The wooden rail splits, gives way, and the two of them fall, hard.

Harper hits the stairs, and the other person falls just below her with a thud. She pushes herself up, feeling pain all down one side of her chest, across her ribs. Her left forearm tingles as if electricity is coursing through it. But she manages to get up at the same time her attacker reveals himself.

His rapid breathing pushes the white cotton mask in, out, in, out. His eyes glare at her from the crude holes cut into the white material. The belt is around his neck. He is buck naked and cut all over from leaping through the wall at her. There is an axe at his feet, the blade covered in blood.

Harper backs off, coughing on the thick air. She glances to the right. Three steps up, her gun lies beneath the cascading dust. The killer sees it, too. As she makes a dive for it, he comes at her, snarling like an animal, his strong hands finding her skin and pinching so hard she thinks he'll tear holes in her body. Harper screams, reaches out for the gun, her fingertips barely scraping the bottom of the handle.

The killer claws his way up to her, and when he's close enough, she realizes there's nothing else to do. She sinks her teeth into his chest. He screams, a high-pitched wail, and pushes himself off her, rolling away and hitting the banisters. Harper grabs her gun, aims it at him.

The man shoves Harper's hand away as she fires, and it goes wide, the sound of it like thunder.

The killer wrestles with Harper for the gun, trying to tear it free from her hands, all the while managing to hold it far enough away from him. They end up lengthwise across the stairs, him on top of her. Harper uses what energy she can muster and shoves to the left. They tumble down the steps, the impact of each stair punching her straight in the ribs. She lands on top of him at the bottom and sees that Ida is watching from the front door.

The man thrusts upward with his hips and sends Harper rolling over him, landing in a heap against the wall. Grunting, he clambers up the stairs and grabs the handle of his axe.

He turns.

Ida blinks, backing off one step, then two. The killer cocks his head inquisitively from one side to the other as he takes her in.

"Ruby?"

Ida looks down at her feet. The gun has clattered along the hall to land next to her. Eyes on the man in front of her, she stoops down and picks it up.

He shakes his head. Reaches up, tears his mask away. Blood dribbles from one side of his mouth. The killer walks toward her, the axe dragging behind him, scraping on the floor.

"You killed my mamma."

That makes him stop. Ida has never fired a weapon. The weight of it, held in front of her, clutched in both hands, is something completely alien to her. She points it at his chest, hoping that her aim won't be too far off. Her finger caresses the trigger. It feels impossible to press down on it, releasing death.

"I loved her," he says, coming for her. "I love 'em all."

Ida looks at Stu's body on the floor, at Harper watching her with one eye open, looking as though she's not far from death's door herself.

"You destroyed them," Ida says. She pulls the trigger. The gun jumps in her hand, and the shot goes wild, punching a hole in the wall. The killer flinches away.

"Ida! Give me the gun!" Harper yells.

As the man rounds back on her, Ida skims the sidearm along the floor. Harper catches it neatly, leveling the weapon on the killer.

She fires just as he turns to face her. The bullet strikes Lester square in the chest and he is blown back, landing against the bottom steps. The axe falls from his limp hand as he slides to a sitting position, attempts to move, then falls facedown on the floor, blood bubbling up from his nose.

Ida rushes to Harper's side. Harper is trembling, the gun still clutched tight in her hand, pointed at Lester Simmons's inert form.

Harper looks at her, panting—her breath coming in ragged gasps. "Ida . . . we need to teach you how to shoot a gun."

In a daze, Ida looks back at the killer. "I don't think I ever want to touch one again."

"Maybe a good idea," Harper says. "Next time you might shoot a hole in yourself."

Ida stands, barely hearing her. "Keep an eye on him, sugar. Case he's still got fight in him."

Confusion clouds Harper's face until she realizes what Ida is doing. "No! Don't go near him, Ida! He's still alive!"

Ida looks at her with fierce determination. "I have to do this. I have to know," she says, crossing the landing and kneeling down next to him. The blood continues to bubble out of his nose. The fingers of one hand twitch sporadically.

Harper flops back, knowing the fight is lost. She aims the gun at Lester Simmons. "Don't touch him . . ."

"I got no choice."

Ida presses her hands down on Lester Simmons's warm body, and she is taken away, carried on a hurricane of light and shadow, hot and cold. His fading heartbeat is the slowing rhythm of a cosmic metronome . . .

Lester's mother rocking back and forth in her chair, knitting needles clicking as she speaks. "Your daddy hated them niggers. He was KKK through and through, yes sir."

"*Why did he hate 'em, Mama?*"

"*They ain't to be trusted. Gettin' ideas above their station, like they real folk. Cussing and drinking and havin' they kids,*" she says, *rolling her words around in her mouth before spitting them out like poison.*

Lester cocks his head to one side. He is just a boy. "*What's the KKK, Mama?*"

She leans forward. "*Don't matter what it is. You just remember they niggers ain't the same as us, you hear? They need teachin' the right ways, the boundaries of what they can and can't do. Your daddy had the right idea, Lester. He treat 'em like you would a dog. What do you do if a dog gets out of line?*"

Lester fumbles for the answer.

"*You give it a good kickin' that's what!*" *his mother shouts impatiently.* "*You could learn a lot from the way your daddy was, God rest his soul.*"

Lester blushes. "*Ruby's my friend, Mama.*"

She stops what she's doing and slaps him in the mouth. Lester cries out, holding a hand to his lips. "*Mama!?*"

Her snarling face is in his, spit flying from between her broken teeth. "*Don't ever think of one of them as a friend again! You hear me boy? We is better than them. Why, your daddy would be rollin' in his grave to hear you blaspheme in such a way. Now, get outta my sight!*"

Ida can feel the hurt, the shame, the confusion. And now she sees Lester walking home from school and Ruby catching up.

"*Hey, Lester, wait for me.*"

He turns toward her, finger in her face. "*I can't walk home with you no more. My mama say,*" *he spits. The f of every s is heavy and thick.*

Ruby backs off. "*Lester . . .*"

He rushes on ahead of her, waving one arm in frustration. "*I can't hear you!*"

Ida wants to take the young girl in her arms and hold her tight, but she can't. She's left to watch her sobbing in the street, the boy she considered a friend storming off, turning against her for no reason other than the pigment of her skin.

It doesn't end there. *Lester watches her come and go. He thinks of her. Despite what his mother has to say to him, he follows her home sometimes, keeping his distance so that she won't see.*

His mother gives him a chest of his father's old belongings. A worn pair of boots, some army paraphernalia, a knife. He roots through it all. Books, papers, medals, his old leather belt, the same belt Mama would use to "teach that boy some sense," as she liked to say. Lester reads what he can in the Hope's Peak library about the KKK, looking at the pictures mostly—when he tries to read the words, they just swim in front of his eyes like black minnows in a stream of white water. At home one night, he takes his pillowcase and cuts two eyeholes. He puts it on his head, but it just flops around. Lester takes his father's old belt and ties it around his neck. Looking in the mirror, he feels a sense of power. That night, when he masturbates, it is better than ever. And all he can think of is Ruby Lane at school. Her tight curly hair and dark-brown skin.

Years pass. Eventually, he gets a job at the dry cleaner's in town and finds her working there, too. They do not speak, but she glances up at him from time to time. One day, he says hello and she says hello back.

"Forry for how I waf back then," Lester offers one afternoon on their break, both of them drinking a cold Coke out back. "I waf confufed."

Ruby smiles weakly. "Okay, Lester."

He asks her to meet him up at Wisher's Pond for a picnic. Ruby says she will, if she can get a sitter for her kid. She lets him down twice before finally seeing it through. Lester finds her waiting for him under the shade of an old tree, standing in the tall grass.

She doesn't appreciate the mask. She doesn't get it. He feels powerful.

As he forces her down, as he hits her, as he consummates their years of friendship, as he wraps his strong hands around her throat, he can feel the power of what he is and what he is doing.

Ida doesn't have any choice but to watch. It is the dream. It is what she has revisited when she closes her eyes, for so, so long. She watches as Lester strangles her mother, then crowns her head with the twisted supplejack vine.

Lester takes a job with an auto repair shop. His mother is at first confined to a wheelchair, then slowly starts to lose her mind. Mack, a man at work he's gotten to know, suggests putting her in a home.

That's what Lester does. He goes to Mack's for dinner and meets his wife, Ceeli. Years later, he has left the repair shop, but he stays in contact with Mack, on and off.

Most of the time, it is Ceeli who calls him when something needs fixing. And when his mother dies, it is Ceeli who gives him comfort. She tells him he can come visit her, have a coffee and a chat, tries to help him through his grief. Lester asks Mack if that will be alright, and Mack doesn't object. A few days after his mother's funeral service, Lester arrives at Ceeli's door.

That's when it starts. Lester tells her how much he misses his mother. Ceeli confides in him that Mack works long hours, sometimes works away, and she gets awful lonely in the house by herself.

Doesn't Mack understand a woman's got needs?

For a time, his mama's voice goes away. But weeks later, he hears her whispering in the dark corners of the house. When he closes his eyes, she is in his head, looking at him, bugs crawling from her rotten eyeballs, out between her jagged teeth.

The dark creeps in at the edges. Ida feels squeezed on all sides, but she knows she must see it through. Lester is falling from the light, from the glow of life. It is above him, as the sun is when you're underwater, sinking toward the abyss.

Before his mama goes to the home, a man comes to the house, dressed in a light-gray suit, with polished brown leather shoes, a pristine white shirt, and a dark-blue tie. He is overweight, has chestnut hair struck through with silver at the sides. He smells like a salesman: cologne, perspiration, and cigar smoke.

He asks if he can come in to speak with him. Lester steps to one side to let him in and the man introduces himself as Hal Crenna. "Maybe you haven't heard of me, but I've known about you for a while. I'm your half brother. We share the same daddy."

Lester shakes his head, stepping back from the man, but it's undeniable. The physical resemblance between the two of them is uncanny. "My daddy's dead . . ."

"That's one way of looking at it."

"Mama ain't never told me about no half brother," Lester mumbles, trying to wrap his head around it. "Like I said, Daddy been in the ground year now."

The man smiles. It makes him look like the devil incarnate. "Weren't your daddy, fella."

"What d'you mean?" Lester asks. He holds the door open for his visitor. "I think you better leave, mister."

"Don't be so hasty." The man produces a photograph. "Here. Have it."

Lester's mama appears at the top of the stairs. "Who's that?"

"Visitor, Mama," Lester calls up. "Says he's my half brother."

His mama's face twists into a furious knot of intense hatred, and she hangs over the banister, pointing one bony claw at their caller. "Don't listen to him, baby!"

"I'll not impose any longer," Hal Crenna says. He heads through the door, then turns back at the threshold. "I'm telling the truth when I say we got the same daddy, Lester. And he's watching over you. We all are. Making sure you don't go getting yourself in trouble so deep you can't pull yourself back out."

Lester knows what he's getting at. The girls. He makes their crown and, after, he gives it to them.

"Lester, get rid of that motherfucker!"

Lester fills the doorway. "I don't know what you're talking about. You better go."

Hal Crenna nods his head in parting. "As you like. But you just watch yourself, Lester. Everyone's got needs, and Lord knows I ain't got nothing against culling a few niggers . . . but watch yourself."

Lester watches him go and wonders if there's any truth to what he's saying. But like most things, the incident is forgotten about soon enough.

Killing once in a blue moon satisfied his urges. But it was never enough. Before long, he was hungry again, yet his mother held him at bay. Her needs, the burden of caring for her in the beginning, was enough to keep him occupied, though he still thought of the girls.

Then, she was admitted to the nursing home and gradually deteriorated. Still, she kept him busy, insisting he visit every day. This left him no time for his girls.

When his mother finally passed, Lester sought solace in the arms of Ceeli, who was eager to give it to him—when Mack was out of town.

The hunger ate away at him. And when he killed, he tasted the lust in his mouth, and he killed again. It was easier. When his mother died, he realized he could finally do as he wanted. He could become the man he'd always wanted to be—the mask had always hidden his true self. He knew that soon he wouldn't need it.

The darkness grows, yawning wide to swallow him whole. Ida lets go, watches him fall, screaming, consumed by the black until there is nothing of him left but the echo of his voice.

A tether snaps, a filament to which Ida was connected with the monster. She is pulled back out of the darkness as surely as he falls toward it.

To the dark ether. Silent and cold. Endless.

Now his scream has faded and there is no sound, nothing but the light growing around her as she surfaces.

Ida remembers telling Harper that death was *warm sunlight from that other place . . . brighter and brighter until there's nothing else.*

But, as she wakes on the floor of the house, Harper asking if she is alright, the smell of gunpowder, death, and sweat filling her nose, the sound of approaching sirens in her ears, the sound of her heart . . . she knows she was wrong. The warm light that pulled her back from oblivion was not death.

It was life.

EPILOGUE

Captain Morelli surveys the scene, John Dudley at his side, coordinating the officers who have arrived to prevent anyone going anywhere near vital evidence.

Morelli looks at where Stu lies in a puddle of his own blood, and he cannot help but feel his heart sink. "Shit."

"He was a good man, sir," Dudley offers.

Morelli glares at him. "I don't think you've got a right to pass comment, son, after what you pulled."

Dudley looks at his shoes. "I suppose you're right."

"Look at me."

Dudley does as he's told.

"I hear Durham has a spot open. I think you're gonna take it. It'd be best all round, don't you think?"

"I—"

Morelli points at Stu. A crime-scene photographer is snapping away, trying to catch the detective from all angles. "That is the price you pay for causing what you did. Be thankful that's all that's happening to you."

The color drains from Dudley's face and he walks outside. Morelli treads carefully around the blood and mess on the floor and hunkers down next to Stu.

"I'm sorry, Detective," he mumbles.

"Harper!" a familiar voice says. She feels someone take her hand, looks down, and sees Albie at the side of the gurney. "Thank God you're okay."

"Thanks, Albie."

"I'm so sorry about Stu," he says. His eyes are rimmed with red, glassy with tears. "I can't believe it."

The paramedics wheel Harper's gurney into the back of the ambulance, jostling her slightly in the process.

"Talk soon," Harper calls to him.

Albie blows her a kiss. Ida elects to travel with her, sitting next to the gurney. The paramedics shut the doors, and the ambulance heads for the hospital, siren wailing.

"You okay, sugar?"

Harper looks at her. "I guess. I can't stop thinking of Stu, though."

"I know," Ida says, taking her hand and squeezing it. "But it'll all make sense tomorrow. And it'll get easier. That hurt you're feelin' right now? You'll get used to it. I did."

"Thank you. Through this whole thing, you've been great."

Ida smiles. There are tears in her eyes. "Don't mention it. Had to be done."

"Hey," Harper says in a hushed voice. "What did you see? When you made the connection with him."

Ida considers telling her, but rethinks it. "Let me tell you in a couple of days, when you're on the mend . . ."

"No, really. I need to know, Ida. What did you see at the end? When he was dying?"

Ida's gaze burns into her as she speaks. "The darkness smothered him like a blanket. I guess he was only darkness all along anyway. That's what he became in the end."

"You saw it?"

Ida nods slowly. "Saw him sink into the black, saw it take him and make him disappear. For people like that, I like to think death is a dark corridor . . . and there ain't no light at the end of it for 'em. Only silence."

The breath seems to catch in Harper's throat and she starts to sob. "And Stu?"

"No, no, no!" Ida smiles, patting her hand. "Trust me, sugar, that boy is surrounded by sunlight. He did good. And maybe I shouldn't tell you this . . ."

Harper frowns. "Tell me what?"

Ida lets go of her hand and reaches over, resting her open palm where Harper's stomach is. "Tell you about the part of him that grows inside you."

Realization dawns on Harper's face.

Ida nods. "You know what I mean."

Harper shakes her head. "I don't believe it . . ."

"Well," Ida says, sitting back and folding her arms. "You better start."

Harper doesn't say anything for a long time. The ambulance bounces on the rough backstreets of Hope's Peak. After the silence has stretched out, and what Ida has told her has sunk in, Harper speaks up. "What will you do now?"

Ida smiles. Her eyes shine. "Sugar, I'm gonna do what I should've done a long time ago. Start living."

Acknowledgments

The author would like to thank the following people for their assistance and support with this book:

Bernard Schaffer, who graciously tore the whole book apart—and helped me put it back together again; David K. Hulegaard and Sandie Slavin, who read the earliest draft and gave their honest feedback; my "Constant Reader" and all-round Irish badass, Barbara Spencer; Meg Gardiner, who gave sound advice when it was needed; my agent, Sharon Pelletier at Dystel & Goderich Literary Management, who took me on as her client and worked tirelessly in getting me a two-book deal; Jacquelyn Ben-Zekry, my editor at Thomas & Mercer, who fell in love with the book and wanted to publish it; and last (but not least) a big thank-you to my wife—without your support I wouldn't have the time, or space, to do what I do. You're my rock.

But of course, the biggest thanks goes to you, dear reader. Having you read these pages means more than you could ever know.

—*TH*

About the Author

Tony Healey is the bestselling author of the Far From Home series. He has written alongside such award-winning authors as Alan Dean Foster and Harlan Ellison.

Tony is currently working on book two of his Harper & Lane series, of which *Hope's Peak* is the first installment. He lives with his wife and four daughters in Sussex, England.